"The panther knew [...] the knowledge ma[...] about him even wh[...] [...]now, Holly was sure he knew it. The panther knew she ate raw meat and licked the blood from her lips . . ."

YEAR OF THE CAT

The terrifying new trilogy by Zoe Daniels

Book One: *The Dream*

When Holly Callison arrives at Los Gatos High School, she learns more than the legend of the panther. She unlocks the secret of her nightmares, the hunger in her soul—and the savage nature of her true self . . .

Book Two: *The Hunt*
(Available in June 1995)

As Holly explores the wild side of her secret destiny, she fears for the lives of the people she loves. But still, she cannot resist the power of the ancient rituals—and the bloodthirsty call of the hunt . . .

Book Three: *The Amulet*
(Available in August 1995)

In terror and desperation, Holly tries to cling to her human side. But the blood of the panther runs wild in her veins. And soon she's forced to choose sides— in the final war between predator and prey . . .

YEAR OF THE CAT

BOOK ONE

The Dream

Zoe Daniels

BERKLEY BOOKS, NEW YORK

YEAR OF THE CAT: THE DREAM

A Berkley Book / published by arrangement with
the author

PRINTING HISTORY
Berkley edition / April 1995

ISBN: 0-425-14768-1

BERKLEY®
Berkley Books are published by The Berkley Publishing Group,
200 Madison Avenue, New York, New York 10016.
BERKLEY and the "B" design
are trademarks belonging to Berkley Publishing Corporation.

PRINTED IN THE UNITED STATES OF AMERICA

10   9   8   7   6   5   4   3   2   1

For my daughter, Anne Laux,
my expert on all things to do with teenagers.
It takes one to know one.

The Dream

Someone was watching her.

Holly Callison was halfway down the main corridor of Los Gatos High School when a shiver like icy fingers ran up her spine and into her shoulders.

Like the feeling you get when someone is watching you.

Holly stopped and looked behind her. There was no one there, nothing in the corridor at all except closed classroom doors and a row of neatly arranged bulletin boards announcing everything from bus schedules to the first school dance of the year. Nothing.

Just to convince herself, Holly let her gaze skim over the corridor again, all the way from where she stood back to the front door she'd just come in.

She hadn't missed a thing.

Closed classroom doors. Bulletin boards. Mural of the school mascot.

Holly got that far and stopped.

She'd noticed the painting when she came in, of course. How could you not notice something that took up the entire wall directly across from the main entrance? But she had so much on her mind, she hadn't given the Los Gatos Panther a second look.

Holly's heart began to beat fast and hard, like a jackhammer inside her ribs.

This was where the uneasy feeling that crept along her shoulders was coming from. She knew it as sure as she knew her own name. Puzzled, she stared at the big cat.

Its huge, black shape was shiny as glass against the duller cream-colored paint that had been used on the rest of the school walls. Too distracted to put on her glasses—or maybe just too vain to wear them, like Mom always said—Holly squinted at the mural. From this angle, she could just make out the silhouette of the sleek cat, its mouth open in a savage snarl, one paw raised, ready for the kill.

Like a billboard seen from a fast-moving car, its details half-remembered, Holly recalled bits and pieces of the picture from when she'd zoomed past.

She had a vague recollection of burning eyes, sharp claws, fangs tipped in blood. "Just your everyday painting of your everyday school mascot." Holly mumbled the words beneath her breath and her mouth twisted into a crooked smile.

"Just your standard man-eater."

Except that she was sure it was watching her.

Holly's smile faded and she clutched the armful of books she was carrying closer to her body.

It was a ridiculous idea, of course. There was no way the eyes of a painting could follow anyone. That kind of thing only happened in old black-and-white movies.

Holly knew it, and she tried to get rid of her fear

with a shake of her head that sent her red hair flying. She was probably just a little out of it from not being able to sleep last night, she reminded herself. She was probably just a little nervous.

Who wouldn't be?

It was her first week in a new town, her first day in a new school. She was anxious to fit in. That's why she'd gotten here so early, to find her homeroom and a few of her classes so she didn't have to wander the corridors like a lost sheep once the bell rang. She was eager not to look too different, or too nervous, or altogether too dumb.

"Great, Callison," she grumbled. "You're worried about looking dumb and you think a painting is watching you. That ought to make a really good first impression!"

Just to prove to herself how silly the whole thing was, Holly traced her steps back to the school's main entrance.

She planted herself squarely in front of the mural and took a good, long look at the panther, starting with its tail.

It was the most logical place to begin, Holly decided, firmly ignoring the little voice in her head that said she was just too chicken to start with the eyes. She would work her way forward, she told herself. In her own sweet time.

The panther's tail was long and slender, held up and out like a warning to its enemies. It led down to the cat's back where its muscles, coiled like powerful springs, bulged just beneath the slick coat of black fur.

Holly swallowed hard and moved her gaze down to the animal's paws. They were huge. She set her books on the floor beside her and held up her right hand, comparing their size.

She did not touch the panther. She didn't want to. Yet Holly was sure she could feel the silky texture of its fur beneath her fingers. It was soft, warm, inviting her closer, and she slid her hand to the left, following the rounded shape of the cat's paw to where it ended in a set of claws sharp as razor blades.

Holly jerked her hand away and stuffed it in the pocket of her jacket.

That's when she noticed that the panther's claws were touched with blood.

A peculiar feeling bubbled up in Holly's stomach. It was like having the flu and being hungry all at the same time. She swallowed, hoping to make the queasy sensation go away.

It wasn't like the blood was real, she told herself over and over. It wasn't like it was anything more than plain old red paint, slapped onto a plain old wall with a plain old paintbrush.

It wasn't like it was real.

After she repeated the words for the twentieth time, the logic of it finally sank in. Holly's stomach settled down. Relieved, she let go of the breath she was holding.

Maybe he wasn't such a scary cat after all, Holly thought. Gulping in another breath for courage, she raised her eyes to those of the panther.

It must have been the shiny paint. Holly swore she

could see her own reflection in the cat's eyes. She blinked back at herself like an owl surprised by a sudden light, her pupils as round as the panther's, her mouth open in surprise. There was a circle of red paint ringing the panther's eyes, and it outlined her lips so that they looked as if she had helped it eat its latest kill.

Look away.

The advice echoed through Holly's thoughts, a sensible voice inside her head that fought against the panic that rooted her to the spot and caused her knees to feel as if they were made out of rubber.

Look away.

But she couldn't.

Holly's gaze locked with the panther's. She leaned closer and her reflection ballooned, until she was one with the cat. Her eyes in his shifted from hazel to green. Her hair turned black as a starless night. Her mouth opened wider, an empty hole except for the two knife-edged fangs of the cat.

She leaned nearer still and, like the stuff of dreams, the mural blurred before Holly's eyes. She couldn't see a thing. Not herself or the cat. Nothing but darkness, absolute and thick. Solid and black. Like the panther's fur.

"You're new here, aren't you?"

Holly jumped and her cheeks got hot when she realized the high, startled shriek she heard came from her. She backed away from the mural and looked around.

There was a dark-haired girl standing next to her

and the corridor was filled with LGH students, laughing and talking, hurrying to their classes.

"I knew you were a first-timer." The girl was a whole head shorter than Holly. She smiled up at her with a friendly expression that brightened her brown, almond-shaped eyes. Dressed in baggy jeans and an oversized denim shirt, her long, dark hair pulled back into a ponytail, the girl looked like someone's kid sister playing high school student. But she seemed to belong. She smiled and waved to just about everyone who walked by.

"That awful thing has that effect on everyone the first time they see it," the girl said. She crossed her eyes and stuck out her tongue at the painting.

"It does?" Holly glanced from the girl to the panther. He didn't look at all mysterious now, not with a noisy bunch of kids all around them getting ready for the first day of school and this spunky little girl making faces at him. He was just a painting and, Holly noted with a scornful smile, not a very good one. She laughed and turned to the girl.

"Holly Callison," she said by way of introduction. "And yes, I am new. We moved here from Cleveland last week. My dad's an art history professor. He's just taken a job at the University."

"Tisha Nakao." Tisha bent and retrieved Holly's books. She handed them to her. "Lifelong Los Gatos resident and self-appointed official junior class busybody. Anything you want to know, just ask."

Before Holly had a chance to even think of anything she wanted to know or ask, Tisha leaned closer and looked her up and down. "You are a junior aren't you?" she asked, and without waiting for an answer, she added, "I figured you were when I saw the way you were dressed."

Holly looked down at her outfit. Anxious to create a good impression, she'd chosen her clothes carefully this morning. Her blue-and-green silk shirt matched her dark blue chinos perfectly. She had always thought blues and greens looked just right with her hair—as right as anything could look with hair the color of sunset—and she glanced up at Tisha, a question in her eyes.

"Oh, you look fabulous!" Tisha gave Holly's arm a friendly squeeze. "I didn't mean to make you think you didn't. You just look . . . well . . ." Tisha searched for the right word. "Sophisticated," she finally said. "Like a junior should."

"Good." Holly let out a sigh.

"Did you mind leaving your old school?" Tisha might have been the leading gossip of the junior class, but Holly could tell her question was not motivated as much by curiosity as it was by concern.

"No," Holly answered quite honestly. "The school was all right and I had a lot of friends, but . . ." She shrugged.

But what?

Not even Holly knew.

She had liked her school in Cleveland well enough and she'd had plenty of friends there, boys and girls. She knew she would always hear from the girls. They'd send funny cards, and pretty little books of poetry at Christmas, and prom pictures, and in a couple years, college dormitory addresses.

And the boys?

The boys would remain what they had always been. Friends. The kind of friends you went to basketball games with, and played softball with, and took home to your mother in spite of the fact that you knew she'd say they were sweet and well-mannered and every mother's idea of what her daughter's friends should be like.

But they weren't boyfriends.

Not the kind you dreamed about. Not the kind who could send your heart thumping with a look and your legs quivering with a kiss. Not the kind of boy she hoped to meet here in Oregon.

"No real boyfriend, huh?"

It was as if Tisha could read minds. Holly felt a wave of heat climb up her neck and into her face. "Nah." She brushed off the confession with a laugh. "Hey, since you know everything and everyone . . ." Only half-teasing, she looked down at Tisha.

"I promise I'll introduce you," Tisha said. "Just let me know when you spot a likely victim. In the meantime, we'd better find your homeroom, the first bell should ring soon."

Holly nodded and Tisha led the way down the corridor.

In spite of her small size—or maybe because of it—Tisha moved like the wind, in and out of the crowd in a flash. Holly had to trot behind to keep up.

"You know, I am an expert on all the really important places in town," Tisha said over her shoulder. "If you've got some time after school, I'll personally show you the best place for pizza."

It was a friendly invitation and Holly accepted it with a smile. "Only if you show me the best place for a hot fudge sundae after," she said.

"It's a deal." Tisha turned into another, longer corridor and stopped in front of the first door. "This is my homeroom," she said. "Which one are you looking for?"

Holly dug through her books until she found the copy of her class schedule. She ran her finger down the list. "Mrs. Green," she said and frowned when Tisha made a face. "Is she bad?"

"The worst!" Tisha laughed in a way that made Holly think maybe Mrs. Green wasn't so bad. "And after that?"

"After that..." Holly checked her list. "Mr. Tollifson for biology."

"Tollifson's a scream," Tisha said. She looked into her homeroom and waved to the students who were already there. "You'll see. Last year he couldn't get enough worms to dissect, so he let his class cut up Twinkies and eat them when they were done. Doesn't do much for your SAT scores, but it sure beats starving until lunchtime!" Tisha pulled a rumpled class schedule from the pocket of her jeans.

"I'm in that class, too," she said. "I'll meet you outside the door before the bell. With any luck we can beat the crowd and sit together."

Before Holly had a chance to agree, a tall, lanky boy poked his head into the hall.

"Hey, Little Bit." He ruffled Tisha's hair. "What's the word on the PNN?"

Tisha clicked her tongue and rolled her eyes, but she didn't look nearly as annoyed to see the boy as she looked pleased. "Haven't you been paying attention, Jason Van Kirk? I told you, it isn't Patty anymore. Patty is a kid's name." Tisha pulled herself up to her full height, which wasn't very high. "It's Tisha now," she said. "I decided over the summer. So much more mature, don't you think?"

"Yeah, mature." Jason nodded, but there was a twinkle in his blue eyes. "So, the PNN has to change to the TNN."

For the first time, Jason looked directly at Holly. He tried to pretend he hadn't noticed her there before, but Holly knew it was only an act. "The Patty News Network becomes the Tisha News Network," he explained with a lopsided smile. "Patty . . . Tisha," he corrected himself, "knows everything." The boy's sandy-colored eyebrows rose to meet the shock of straw-colored hair that fell over his forehead. "And everyone."

"And tells it only to those who are worthy," Tisha piped in, trying her best to keep from smiling.

"I am definitely worthy. And you" —Jason poked Tisha in the arm with one finger— "you still owe me a buck for that bet we had on the Mariners opening game last spring. You didn't think I'd let you forget, did you?" He tipped his head in Holly's direction. "I'll let you skate on the bet if you introduce us."

Tisha agreed with a characteristic laugh. "Jason Van

Kirk," she said. "Jason is the genius behind the 'Cat Calls' column in the school newspaper. He always gets the juiciest interviews."

Jason stepped forward and looked at Holly in a comical imitation of a leer. "And you," he said, "are about as juicy as they get."

Holly couldn't help but laugh.

"This is Holly Callison," Tisha said, laughing, too. "She's new to Los Gatos and new to the school and"— she raised her chin and gave Jason an I-beat-you-to-it look—"she's coming for pizza with me after school, so don't even bother to ask."

Jason's eyes flew open wide. "Me? Would I even think of butting in? I won't even ask where you're going." He raised one hand, Boy Scout–style, and retreated back into his homeroom.

"I don't have to," Jason called out to them after he was around the corner. "I know you'll be at Gino's. I'll meet you there at four."

"Subtle as a three-dollar bill." Tisha shook her head.

"I don't mind," Holly said. "He's kind of cute and he's awfully funny."

The first bell rang. Tisha started into her room and pointed Holly across the hall to her homeroom.

"Thanks. See you in biology." Holly raised her right hand in a friendly gesture.

There was blood on her finger.

Holly stopped in the middle of the corridor and examined her hand. There was a cut along the side of her right index finger, the kind of small, sharp cut caused by paper or the edge of a razor blade. On either side of it, there was a fine trickle of nearly dried blood. Holly rummaged through her purse for a tissue and wrapped it around her finger.

She crossed the hall to her homeroom and sat in the desk nearest the door, dabbing at the wound.

She wondered how it got there.

Alex Sarandon pushed open the front door of Los Gatos High and stopped in his tracks.

There was someone new in school.

He could feel her.

He could smell her.

Every muscle poised, every sense alert, Alex glanced around the nearly empty corridors. The first bell had already rung, he'd heard it while he parked his car. The few kids left in the hallways were mostly freshmen, lost, and looking like they were about to burst into tears.

He dismissed them without a second thought, his lip curling with distaste.

They were new, but they smelled only of anxiety. Not a pleasant scent.

No, this smell was different, an aroma that lingered in the air like the echo of a hunting bird's call—clean, refreshing, exciting.

Alex took a deep breath.

There was no fear in this scent, not the kind he smelled on the freshmen. Only exhilaration. As if the girl who left it was poised on the edge of some new adventure, and couldn't wait to plunge headlong into it.

The short hairs on the back of Alex's neck stood

on end. He felt his heartbeat quicken like it did when he was running the track, racing against the wind. He smiled, a slow, easy smile, and turned to head toward the junior homerooms, certain that was the way the new girl had gone.

"We're supposed to stop at the office first." Exasperated, Laila Sarandon grabbed her brother's sleeve to hold him in place.

Alex had forgotten she was there. In one smooth movement, he spun to face her and snatched her hand from the sleeve of his denim jacket. He held it up, away from him, his fingers tight around her wrist, his expression warning her she had gone too far.

"We're supposed to make the PA announcement for this weekend's football game, remember?" Laila wasn't as annoyed by Alex's behavior as she was baffled by it. She yanked her hand out of his grasp. "You don't remember anything, do you?" she asked with a toss of her head that sent her long black hair slithering over one shoulder. "You—"

Laila raised her head and sniffed the air. Her nostrils flared. Her green eyes widened. She darted a look down the corridor, down to the junior homerooms. "Or weren't you even thinking about the football game?" she asked, her voice suddenly sharp with suspicion.

The tips of Alex's fingers prickled, the way they always did when someone irritated him. He ran his thumbs over the ends of his fingers, willing the reaction away. He looked down at his sister. Being twins with a girl like Laila wasn't so bad usually. Except at times like this.

At times like this, Alex almost wished he didn't have a twin who shared his looks as well as his instincts.

He pushed the thought away.

"You do the announcement without me." Alex turned and started toward the junior homerooms, eager to be away from his sister and the disturbing emotions she was so good at bringing to the surface. "I've got something to do."

Laila never moved. She watched him carefully. Alex could feel the look bore straight through the back of his jacket.

"Yes," Laila said. Though Alex was already halfway down the hall, she spoke in a whisper. It was meant for his ears alone and he heard her loud and clear above the distracting noises around him.

"Yes," Laila said again, hanging on to the last bits of the word so that it hissed like a snake in his ears. "I'll just bet you do."

2

"Mushrooms and green peppers." Tisha licked her lips.

"Black olives," Holly added.

"Onions," Jason said. "And pepperoni and—"

"No pepperoni," Holly blurted out before the waitress could write it down. She gave her friends a hesitant smile. "I'm a vegetarian."

"Right." Jason accepted her announcement readily enough. With a quick smile of apology to the waitress, he adjusted their order. "Okay, no pepperoni. Add some hot peppers instead."

Holly sank back against the imitation leather of Gino's booth and twirled her napkin through her fingers. She felt she owed Tisha and Jason some sort of explanation simply because they were being so understanding. "Well, I'm not exactly an official vegetarian," she said. "I used to eat some meat. Back in Cleveland. But I've been thinking about becoming a vegetarian for a while. I figured it was as good a time as any to go cold turkey, what with a new town and new friends and—"

"And you don't need to explain." Jason leaned forward and refilled Holly's glass from the pitcher of

Coke on the table. "We're friends. We make concessions to each other's tastes. I can't stand it when Tisha eats that raw fish and tofu salad that her grandmother makes—"

"And I gag whenever Jason brings peanut butter and banana sandwiches for lunch." Tisha added. "We'll be happy to ignore your weird eating habits, if you ignore ours."

"Consider it done." Holly smiled at her two new friends. "I can't believe we just met this morning. I feel like I've known you guys for years."

Tisha laughed. "Oh, it'll seem like years once you hear Jason's collection of corny jokes a couple dozen times."

"Hey, that reminds me." Jason's blue eyes lit with mischief. "Have you heard the one about—"

Holly and Tisha both groaned. They wadded their napkins into balls and threw them at Jason.

Trying his best to look indignant—and failing miserably—Jason glanced around the restaurant. "Well, if that's the way you feel," he said, "I'll have to find someone who appreciates my humor and intelligence." He smiled when he saw a heavyset boy wearing glasses, who was sitting at a table on the other side of the room.

"Ah, Ben Wiley, the editor of the school newspaper. I want to tell him I'm all set to do that column on new students." Jason stood and winked at Holly. "And I know just who my first interview is going to be."

Holly leaned back in the booth, her gaze following

Jason as he walked across the room, her lips parted in a smile. "He's so nice."

"Yeah, nice." Tisha watched Jason sit down with Ben before she turned her attention back to Holly. "Something tells me that's not the way he'd like you to think about him."

"Don't be silly. We just met." Holly brushed her hair away from her face and tucked it behind her ears. "He hardly knows me and—"

"And you don't know Jason Van Kirk the way I do." Tisha poured herself another Coke. "I haven't seen him this eager to impress a girl in a long time. He's nuts about you. Can't you tell? He's practically falling over himself trying to make you laugh."

"It's working. I think he's hilarious." Holly took a sip of her drink.

Tisha was sitting next to Holly. She propped both her elbows on the table and turned to her. She gave Holly a questioning look. "But?"

"But nothing. He's the kind of guy you would take home to Mom, if you know what I mean. Perfectly nice. Perfectly harmless."

Tisha made a face. "Nice and harmless isn't good enough for you? You haven't met some of the creeps in the junior class who actually pass as human beings. Jason's a find, believe me. You're lucky you haven't met Joe Barnes yet. Or Charlie Nakamura." She jiggled her shoulders and Holly was reminded of a dog that had just come in from the rain and was eager to get rid of every last raindrop trapped in its fur.

"Creeps. Both of them. And my grandmother would

love to see me date Charlie just because she knows his grandmother. Why, do you know, last year at the homecoming dance . . ."

Tisha continued to talk as Holly had learned only Tisha could. She really was an encyclopedia of gossip. She knew everything about everyone in the junior class. But by the time Tisha finished her homecoming story and started another about the final day of school last year, Holly's mind began to wander.

It wasn't that she didn't care what Tisha was talking about. It would be a definite advantage to know the inside information on her fellow classmates before she ever met them. But while Tisha was talking, the door to Gino's snapped open. A short, good-looking boy poked his head into the restaurant. He looked around as if he were checking to see if the coast was clear.

Intrigued, Holly watched.

Whatever the boy saw, it obviously met his approval. He pushed the door open and stood back, like a doorman moving aside to usher in a queen.

By this time, Holly's thoughts were a million miles away from whatever Tisha was saying. Her attention was riveted to the interesting little scene being played out at Gino's door.

Natural curiosity, she told herself. But there was nothing natural or normal about the strange flutter of emotion that rocketed through her as she watched the empty doorway.

It was the kind of feeling you had when you were a kid and you were getting ready for trick-or-treating on Halloween night, Holly decided.

Excited.

Like you felt for days ahead of time when you were talking to your friends about what you were going to wear, which houses you were going to visit.

Impatient.

Like you felt when you were slipping into your homemade costume and smearing gooey makeup on your face.

Scared.

Like you felt when you were standing at the front door, ready to leave. You couldn't wait to get going even though you knew it was more than likely there'd be something out on the dark streets that was going to scare you silly.

This was excitement, pure and simple, and it tingled through Holly's veins like the bubbles that danced up the sides of her soda glass. Her heart thumping, she kept her gaze fastened to the empty doorway.

It didn't stay empty for long.

Two girls walked into the restaurant.

No. Holly corrected herself. *Walked* wasn't nearly the right word. They didn't walk. They pranced, like thoroughbred horses or fashion models on a Paris runway.

They looked like models, too. Both of them. Their clothes were perfect. Their hair was gorgeous. Their skin glowed.

As if a pinprick burst the bubble of her excitement, Holly felt the peculiar quiver of anticipation inside her evaporate. Certainly there was nothing about either of these girls that could have justified the feeling.

She sat back, baffled, and she had to admit, more than a little disappointed. She had never believed in premonitions or omens, never supposed that a shiver across the shoulders meant someone was walking over your grave or that your ears burned when someone was talking about you.

Yet this funny feeling had seemed so real, so sure. At least for that one brief second. It had seemed so right and so exciting, Holly had been ready to believe.

It was embarrassing to know just how gullible she could be.

The realization left a sour taste in Holly's mouth. She washed it away with another drink of soda and watched the girls settle down in a large, horseshoe-shaped booth along the far wall. They were joined by the boy who had opened the door and another boy who was tall and fair-skinned and as beautiful as a picture in one of her dad's Renaissance painting books.

A moment later, another girl came into Gino's.

At the first sight of her, the peculiar buzz began again in Holly's veins. Her fingers tingled and she ran them over the plastic tablecloth, hoping to drive away the itch. She sat up straighter, fascinated.

The girl was no taller than Holly herself, five foot six, maybe five foot seven, but she walked with all the dignity of a queen. Her head was up, her shoulders were back. Her slim hips swayed with every graceful movement.

Her face wasn't as beautiful as it was unusual. Her cheekbones were high. Her nose was straight and slender. Her lips were full, with just a hint of red. Her chin was square, full of confidence and, Holly imagined, more than just a trace of stubbornness.

The girl's eyes were narrow and pointed, like a cat's, and as she turned to look around the room, Holly saw that they were just as green. Her hair was black. It fell well past her shoulders, as sleek and shiny as a splash of drawing ink.

She looked like she owned the world.

The thought crossed Holly's mind. But only for a moment.

The next second, a boy walked into the restaurant and every rational thought went flying out of Holly's head.

At the first sight of him, the peculiar feeling inside Holly intensified until it filled every inch of her and caused her blood to throb in her ears.

Holly looked from the dark-haired girl to the boy. They must be twins. No two people could look so much alike and not be.

But if the girl looked like she owned the world, her brother looked as if he ruled it.

He didn't smile, or glance around. He moved to the table where his friends were sitting like Holly imagined a king would move through his kingdom, eyes forward, head straight. His expression was as proud and self-assured as the way he walked.

There was a certain savage energy in every one of his movements, the kind of barely contained power Holly remembered seeing in football players who'd been taken out of the game. They paced the sidelines like animals in their cages, eager to be part of the action, anxious to get back into the fight. Yet this boy's movements were more elegant than any athlete's she had ever seen—smooth and so controlled, Holly could tell every one was calculated for efficiency as well as for effect.

He shared his sister's looks as well as her coloring. But the features that made the girl's face merely unusual made him drop-dead handsome. It helped that he was at least six feet tall and that his shoulders were broad.

The tight-fitting jeans didn't hurt, either.

Holly fanned the heat from her face with one hand.

The boy slipped out of his denim jacket and hung it on the nearest coat peg. He was wearing a black T-shirt that emphasized the muscles in his chest and arms. They looked as firm and well-defined as those of the statues she had seen at the University's museum where her dad worked.

The boy turned, ready to slide into the booth. At the last second, he caught himself and straightened. Though Holly could swear she hadn't heard a thing, the boy tilted his head as if he'd heard someone call his name. He glanced around the restaurant, the look intense and piercing. It brushed everyone in the room, searching, probing, and came to a stop on Holly.

His eyes were as green as summer leaves and as cold as ice. They held hers for a second. Two. His lips turned up at the corners in the smallest of smiles.

A hot flush crept up Holly's face and into her cheeks. Still, she couldn't turn her eyes away. Not even when the thrill in her veins turned into a full-fledged jolt that blasted through her like an electric shock, one that left her hands trembling and sent her heart into her throat.

It was over as quickly as it started.

Holly blinked back from whatever spell held her. The boy was sitting at the table, talking and laughing with his friends.

"Who is he?" Her voice lowered to a rough whisper, Holly grabbed Tisha's arm.

Tisha stopped talking in the middle of a sentence. "Huh?"

"Who is he?" Holly asked again. The urgency of her request made her voice sound shrill and so strange that Tisha stared at her, her face clouded with confusion.

It couldn't have taken more than a couple seconds for Tisha to figure out what Holly was talking about, but it felt like an eternity. Holly squirmed in her seat. Her purse was sitting next to her, and Holly scooped it up and unzipped it. She fished inside for her glasses case. Praying she didn't look too conspicuous, she perched her glasses on the end of her nose and cast one glance toward the other side of the restaurant, another much more meaningful one at Tisha.

"Oh." Tisha bent at the waist to look past Holly. She nodded her understanding. "Oh, that he," she said.

"Yes, that he." Holly took a drink of her soda, using the opportunity to look straight across the room from over the rim of her glass. She gave Tisha's arm a small shake. "He's even better looking with my glasses on! Will you tell me already? The suspense is killing me!"

"That's Alex Sarandon." Tisha didn't sound nearly as enthusiastic as Holly expected her to be. The catch in her voice caused Holly to turn to her.

Tisha didn't look any more interested than she sounded. Her lips were pinched at the corners. Her dark brows were low over her eyes. "That's his sister, Laila, he's sitting next to, and all the rest of their little clique."

Tisha looked down the length of the booth and her frown deepened. "Amber and Raymond," she said, indicating one of the first girls who'd walked in and the boy who had held the door. "Lindsey and Tom." That was the second girl and the handsome blond boy. "Laila and Alex." She sat back against the booth with a grunt of disapproval. "You don't want to know any more."

"But I do." Holly whipped off her glasses and tossed them back into her purse.

She wanted to know more. She needed to know more. But how could she explain all that to Tisha?

How could she describe the shock of awareness that shot through her the first time she saw Alex? How could she tell Tisha about the tiny flame that seemed to sizzle in her stomach even now, long after he'd turned his attention back to his friends? How could she explain—how could she possibly explain—that something deep inside her made her certain that Alex had felt all the same things?

There were no words she could use. Rather than

try to explain, Holly decided to play on Tisha's sympathies. "You did promise you'd introduce me," Holly reminded her. "Remember? This morning? You said you'd introduce me as soon as I found a likely victim."

Tisha crossed her arms over her chest. "I didn't mean Alex. He's not a likely victim. Concentrate on Jason. You'll have much better luck and you won't have to put up with Laila." Her nose wrinkled as she mentioned the girl's name. "You'll be better off, believe me."

Holly ran one finger through the wet ring left on the table by her glass. She looked up at Tisha with the look her dad had come to call the "puppy dog stare": lower lip extended, eyes sad and pitiful, chin drooping with defeat.

Tisha let out a sharp breath. She was obviously not as susceptible to the look as Dad always was. She held her ground. "Even if I could, I wouldn't," she said. She raised her chin and gave Holly the kind of look that said she could be just as bullheaded as Holly was being. "And I probably won't have to. I hear they're both in our biology class. They probably would have been there today if they weren't so busy playing king and queen of the school. You're better off staying far away from that bunch. They're nothing but trouble."

"Who are we talking about?" Jason slid into his seat just in time to grab the first piece of pizza as it was delivered to the table. "Not the Royal Family?" He tipped his head toward where Alex and Laila were seated.

"Tisha doesn't like them." Holly reached for a piece of pizza and continued talking. She thought Tisha would protest, but she didn't. Tisha didn't say a word. She snatched a piece of pizza from the serving dish and sat there staring at it.

That was fine with Holly; it gave her a chance to work on Jason.

"She won't tell me anything about Laila and Alex," she said.

"What's to tell?" Chewing the last bite of his first piece of pizza, Jason reached for a second. "Laila's the queen of the school. Always has been. She's head of the cheerleaders. Star of the drama club productions. No one can touch her when it comes to looks, personality and popularity. She's the main mover and shaker in her own little sorority."

Jason put a strange emphasis on the last word, and Holly looked at Tisha, hoping she would explain.

"It's not a genuine sorority," Tisha said. Her tone of voice made it clear that she would rather be talking about something else. Anything else. She picked a hot pepper off her pizza and tossed it onto Jason's dish. "Nothing official. Just a group of girls who hang out together. Amber and Lindsey are the two leading members, but there are a couple others, too. Carole Harrison's one. And Annie Gillet and Becky Shuster. Anybody who's anybody. The cream of the junior class. You can forget about belonging," she said with a sidelong look at Holly, "unless you shop at all the right stores, wear all the right clothes, and live in the one and only rich neighborhood in Los Gatos."

"Meow!" Jason's cat imitation sounded more like a cross between a steam locomotive and a squeaky door. Reaching for the shaker of hot pepper seeds that sat next to the sugar packets in the middle of the table, he shook a heaping portion onto the next piece of pizza he grabbed, and took a bite.

"And you think guys have ego problems!" he said between mouthfuls. "You girls are a catty bunch! Jealousy, that's what it is. Just because Laila and her friends happen to be the most gorgeous girls in the school—" He looked at Holly. "Present company excluded, of course. Just because they're the most popular, and the best dressed, and the best looking—"

"That's not why I don't like them and you know it, Jason." Tisha didn't seem to be enjoying her pizza. She hadn't taken a bite. "I don't like them," she said to Holly, "because they're snooty. Can't you tell just by looking at them? They treat the rest of us kids in school like we're a species below them. Especially Laila."

Holly finished her piece of pizza and yanked a clean napkin from the metal holder. She wiped her fingers before she reached for another piece. "And what about her brother?" she asked, trying her best to keep her voice casual. She knew she wouldn't get an unbiased answer from Tisha, so she turned to Jason. "Is he just like Laila?"

"Alex?" His mouth full, Jason considered the question. He swallowed and took an enormous drink of soda. "Alex is all right," he said. "He's not unfriendly."

"But he's not friendly, either," Tisha broke in.

"He doesn't need to be." Jason reached for another slice of pizza. "He's nice enough when you meet him in the hallways or out on the track. Always says hello. Besides, he's co-captain of the football team and everybody knows he'll win the election for junior class president in a couple weeks. He's got plenty of friends."

"Plenty of girlfriends," Tisha grumbled under her breath.

"Love 'em and leave 'em." Jason's smile was supposed to be sophisticated and a little lustful. He was a lousy actor. His eyes betrayed the fact that he didn't mean a word he was saying.

"That's how I'm going to be someday," he said. "A girl for every day of the week. Two for Saturdays and Sundays."

This, at least, was enough to bring the hint of a smile back to Tisha's face. Holly suspected that was exactly why Jason had said it. "You couldn't find one girl who'd have you," Tisha said with her best attempt at a sneer. "None of them are nuts enough to put up with you."

"They just can't fathom my genius." Jason leaned back in the booth and patted his stomach. It definitely looked rounder than when they'd come into Gino's. A full stomach and the contentment that went along with it obviously made him feel like causing trouble. He gave Tisha a sly look. "Tell Holly the real reason," he said. "Why you really don't like Laila and Alex."

Tisha ignored him. She tore off a bite of pizza and chomped it in silence.

The brief rest had obviously been just enough to recharge Jason's hunger. Still watching Tisha carefully, he sat up and scooped another piece of pizza from the serving dish. He bit into it with enthusiasm and leaned over the table toward Holly. "She doesn't want you to know about the legend," he whispered.

Tisha tossed her piece of pizza onto her plate. Her face went as hard as a mask.

Holly looked from Tisha to Jason. There was nothing but playfulness in Jason's expression. He was teasing Tisha, and having fun. What he didn't realize was that Tisha was taking him seriously. Her hands were clenched on her lap, her jaw was rigid.

Holly tried her best to change the subject. "Did anybody write down our biology assignment? I know we're supposed to read chapter one, but—"

"Go ahead. Tell her about the legend." Jason wasn't about to let the game end. He hunched up one shoulder and screwed his face into a grotesque imitation of the hunchbacked servant in every bad monster movie ever made. "Go ahead," he said, taking in a sloppy, noisy breath. "Tell Holly how Laila and Alex remind you of the brother and sister in the legend, the twins who were killed by the Los Gatos Panther. Tell her how you can sometimes still see the ghost of the panther out near the old camp at the edge of town."

"It isn't funny." Tisha jumped to her feet so quickly, she nearly tipped over the table.

Jason steadied it at the same time Holly reached

out a hand toward Tisha. "He was only kidding," she said.

"Hey, Little Bit, I didn't mean to upset you." The devilish smile was gone from Jason's face. He looked as sorry as a little boy who'd just broken his mother's best lamp. "I was just teasing. You know I was. I—"

"Yeah." Tisha offered Jason and Holly a weak smile. She dropped back into her seat. "I know. It's just that . . . it's something you shouldn't make fun of. You know what my grandmother says about that area around the old camp."

"Yeah, that it's haunted." Jason laughed. His hand already on the last piece of pizza, he caught himself. He slid the serving dish toward the girls. "Do you guys want—"

Holly and Tisha shook their heads.

Jason grabbed the pizza before they could change their minds. "I know," he said, his mouth full, "I shouldn't make fun of the supernatural. I can't help it." He smiled, one corner of his mouth shiny with pizza sauce. "I'm just that kind of guy! Ghosts don't stand a ghost of a chance with me. And as for legends—"

"You're a legend in your own mind." This time, it was Tisha who was trying to steer the conversation in a different direction.

Holly followed her lead. "Yeah, I don't think I've ever seen anyone eat so much."

"Me?" Jason looked around as if there were some possibility they were talking about someone else. "Did

I eat a lot? I was just going to ask you guys if you wanted to order another pizza."

He looked at them hopefully.

"It's almost dinnertime," Tisha reminded him.

The idea obviously appealed to Jason. The bill was sitting on the table along with the money they'd all carefully counted out. Jason called the waitress over and slid the money toward her. He was out of his seat and almost to the door before Holly and Tisha could get their purses and jackets together.

"Wouldn't want to miss dinner," Jason said over his shoulder to them. "My mom's making pot roast."

Holly and Tisha laughed. They were still laughing when they passed the table where Alex Sarandon was sitting.

Holly felt her smile go rigid at the same time the buzzing got louder in her head. The closer she got to Alex, the more the blood pounded through her veins.

He didn't look up. He didn't pay the slightest attention to her.

He didn't have to.

The nearer she got to him, the more certain Holly became.

This was it.

Alex Sarandon was what she'd been waiting for.

3

He didn't even know she was alive.

Holly propped one elbow on her desk and cradled her chin in her hand.

Two weeks ago when she first saw him, she'd been so sure. She was convinced that when Alex Sarandon looked at her, he felt the same thrill of excitement she felt when she saw him. She was certain his heart was beating just as fast, positive he was just biding his time, waiting for the right moment to introduce himself and make his feelings known.

Holly sighed. She pretended she was watching Mr. Tollifson at the front of the biology room.

Two weeks ago was two weeks ago, she reminded herself. This was now. The realization settled in Holly's stomach like a lump of ice. Now, she was convinced Alex didn't even know she was alive.

They'd passed in the halls a time or two, but he never spoke to her. He never looked at her, even though he was in this class and her history class, too. He never even acknowledged her existence. He was always too busy with his own friends and the small circle of adoring girls who followed him around like lovesick puppies. The only way she knew any of them realized she even existed was because Laila gave her dirty looks once in a while.

Holly frowned down at her biology workbook. She was supposed to be taking notes, but instead the page in front of her was covered with meaningless doodles: hearts and flowers, a house with a tree out front and smoke coming from its chimney, the initials "AS" that she'd scrawled across the page and then crossed out, in case anyone should see them.

She glanced up. Mr. Tollifson was drawing a picture of a flatworm and labeling its parts. Holly moved her pencil over the page, mechanically copying the diagram, fitting the picture between the house doodle and a particularly sappy cluster of frilly hearts. Her mind was about as far from flatworms as it was possible to get. It was right where she found her gaze wandering again and again.

Right on Alex Sarandon.

From this angle in the last row of lab stations, Holly could just see the back of Alex's head. He was seated in the next row over, three seats farther toward the front. He was bent over his work, and she watched the muscles in his neck ripple as he wrote in his notebook, his hand moving along the page quickly, trying to keep up with Mr. Tollifson's brisk explanation.

Checking what Mr. Tollifson was putting on the board, Alex looked up. Holly studied his silhouette. A stab of sunlight flowed through the classroom windows and brought out blue-black highlights in his hair.

She wondered how it would feel to run her fingers through it.

The thought caught Holly off guard and she sucked in a sharp breath, trying to chase it away. It was no use. The more she thought about it, the more appealing the idea seemed. She slid her pen along her notebook page, casually sketching the one errant curl of inky hair that tumbled over the back of Alex's shirt collar.

The drawing was finished in less than a minute. The fact that it was pretty good didn't surprise Holly at all. She'd always been a better than average artist, good enough to consider majoring in commercial art once she entered college. What was surprising was the way the sketch reminded her of the mural out in the hall, the painting of the Los Gatos Panther.

It must have been the shape. The curl of Alex's hair that she'd drawn was sleek and curved, like the outline of the panther. And she'd used her darkest pencil, so it was just as black. Even the angle at which she'd positioned the sketch on her page reminded her of the way the panther was poised on the wall, its tail held up and back, one paw raised to attack.

It needed eyes, and a muzzle, and fangs, of course. She sketched them in, her pencil flying over the page.

Holly stared down at the results.

It wasn't an exact duplicate of the panther, but it was close enough. Close enough to send a skitter of panic up her spine.

She'd almost forgotten the strange effect the panther mural had on her the first day of school. It seemed like a thousand years ago. Now, the memory came back at full force, knocking Holly's breath away. Trying to hide from the picture and all the frightening memories it brought to mind, she flipped the page of her notebook quickly.

Too quickly.

The notebook slid across the lab table and hit the floor with more noise than she imagined a notebook could make.

Holly cringed. Too embarrassed to look around to see if anyone had noticed, she bent to retrieve her notebook. It had landed just out of reach and she leaned farther out into the aisle, her one hand clenched around the edge of the table to keep herself from falling, the other reaching out for the notebook.

She was still balanced between the lab station and the floor when she heard Mr. Tollifson call her name.

"Ms. Callison?" The biology teacher was a short man, and as round as he was tall. From this angle, all Holly could see were the tips of his sensible penny loafers and the bottoms of his brown polyester pant legs.

She saw him raise himself up on the balls of his feet and she knew he was peering down at her just like she'd seen him peer down at countless others who had made major blunders in his class. She knew his glasses would be at the end of his nose. His bald head would be gleaming in the light. His face would be quivering with an expression halfway between annoyance and disbelief.

"Ms. Callison? Do you have something to share with us?"

Holly pulled herself back into her chair.

Mr. Tollifson was looking at her, all right. So was everyone else. Including Alex. He had turned in his seat and he was watching her carefully, a small grin brightening the edges of his expression.

Holly's face was bright red. She knew it was. Her ears burned, her cheeks felt like fire. They got even hotter when she realized Alex's smile was widening with every passing second.

She squirmed in her seat. "No." Her voice was rough with embarrassment. Holly cleared her throat. "No," she said again, fighting to put at least some composure back in her voice. "Not a thing."

Mr. Tollifson nodded, his egg-shaped head bobbing up and down. He was a good teacher. But he was also the toughest teacher Holly had ever had. He demanded attention in his class. Throwing a notebook to the floor, Mr. Tollifson's expression seemed to say, was not acceptable behavior, and he wasn't about to let her off easily.

His hands behind his back, Mr. Tollifson rose up on his toes and pinned Holly with a look. "I thought perhaps you had something to say about the dietary habits of flatworms."

"Flatworms . . ." Holly coughed politely. "What they eat . . ." She dared a look around at the sea of faces watching her.

Mr. Tollifson was waiting for an answer. He looked impatient.

Jason was sitting on the other side of the room. He read her like a book. He knew she hadn't been paying the least bit of attention and now he knew she'd been caught. He was trying so hard not to laugh, his cheeks were bright red.

Laila was directly in front of Holly. She tossed her head and turned in her seat, bored by the whole thing.

Tisha was sitting next to Holly. She looked nearly as embarrassed as Holly herself.

Alex . . . For a split second, Holly considered the expression on Alex's face. Alex, she decided, looked fascinated. Perhaps it was a trick of the light, but Holly could have sworn he winked at her.

"Maybe she isn't sure which flatworms you're talking about." It was Alex's voice she heard, Alex who came to her rescue, and Holly let go a ragged breath and watched in stunned silence.

Alex turned toward the front of the room, effectively diverting attention from Holly. He leaned back in his chair, one arm casually thrown over the back. "If you mean turbellarians," he said, "well, they're free-living. They're usually found in the sand and mud at the bottom of lakes, and they eat what they find there. But if you're talking about the other flatworms, they're parasites and—"

His explanation was interrupted by the bell.

"Saved by the bell." Tisha crumpled in her chair like a discarded accordion.

"You mean saved by Alex Sarandon," Holly mumbled under her breath.

It was still almost too much to believe. The thought of what Alex had done for her caused a curious, comfortable warmth to fill Holly's insides.

Taking a moment to compose herself, she put on her best smile. She turned back to where Alex was sitting, ready to offer him her thanks.

He was already out the door.

• • •

" . . . so if you'd go to homecoming with me . . ."

For somebody who was so easygoing most of the time, Jason looked like he was about to fall through the floor.

He stood at the head of the cafeteria table where Holly and Tisha were sitting, shifting nervously from foot to foot. His gaze was fastened to the squares of green and white linoleum at his feet. His voice trembled. His face, what Holly could see of it, was red from the tip of his dimpled chin to the roots of his hair. He hadn't even finished his lunch—Holly looked over to the next table where three peanut butter and jelly sandwiches sat untouched next to the four cartons of milk Jason had bought to go with them—and that was a sure sign he wasn't feeling right.

"I mean . . . you know . . . the bonfire the night before the game. And the game. And the homecoming dance." Jason looked at her from beneath the shock of sandy-colored hair that always seemed to be falling over his forehead. "Will you?"

Holly couldn't say she hadn't been expecting it. She glanced at Jason, a tight smile pasted to her face. Even though it wasn't for a while yet, she knew he was going to ask her to homecoming, and she'd been practicing her response. Yet somehow, now that the time had come to accept Jason's invitation, she couldn't bring herself to do it.

She looked over Jason's shoulder. Alex and his crowd were having lunch at a table nearby. Holly felt a brief stab of disappointment. In spite of what she'd been hoping, in spite of what had happened in biology class this morning, she knew Alex had no intention of asking her to homecoming.

Feeling more than a bit guilty that she'd ever let the ridiculous idea enter her mind, she turned her attention back to Jason. "I'd like very much to go to homecoming with you," she said. She felt even more ashamed when she saw how her answer caused Jason's face to crack into a wide smile. His nervousness dissolved and he flopped down in the chair next to Holly's.

"Would you? Really? That's great. I mean, it's excellent. I mean it's . . . it's . . ."

"It's about time you asked." Tisha was watching them like a fan at a tennis match, her eyes shifting back and forth between Holly and Jason. "It took you long enough. The game is next Friday."

"You're going, aren't you?" Holly asked Tisha.

Tisha's dark eyes sparkled. "Zack Wright asked me this morning." She gave Jason a look that said he had nearly spoiled her fun. "I didn't want to tell you until Prince Charming here got up the nerve to ask you."

"Then we can go together!" Holly felt a grin tickle the corners of her mouth. She was glad she'd accepted Jason's invitation. She knew she and Jason would have a great time, and they could double with Tisha and Zack, which would make it twice the fun.

Jason grabbed his lunch. He finished the first sandwich in record time and started in on the second. "I'll drive Thursday night," he told them. "And Friday, too, if you want. You don't want to take my old clunker to the dance if you girls are going to be all dressed up. Let's see . . ." He chewed thoughtfully. "The bonfire starts at eight, so I'll pick up Zack first. He lives closest to me. Then we'll come get you, Holly, and Tisha, we'll come for you last."

"Oh, no." Tisha shook her head. "I'll be happy to tag along with you guys to the game and the dance, but there's no way I'm going on Thursday. If you were smart, you'd stay home, too." She sat back, the action as final as her statement.

Holly watched as the excitement on Tisha's face dissolved. There was something going on here, something Holly didn't understand at all. She only knew that whatever it was, it disturbed Tisha. She turned to Jason, a question in her eyes.

"Tisha doesn't want to go to the bonfire," Jason explained, "because it's always held up on Harper's Mountain."

That was about as much help as nothing.

Holly drummed her fingers on the table, waiting for more.

The rest of the story finally came from Tisha. "The bonfire's always held up near the old camp," she said, darting a look at Jason that clearly said she didn't appreciate having to explain this herself. "In a place called Panther Hollow. That's up on Harper's Mountain. And there's no way on earth I'm going up there at night."

A dim memory made its way through Holly's brain. Something someone had said that first day at Gino's. She felt a laugh start to gurgle up in her. Certain she would offend Tisha, she controlled it. "You mean because of the legend of the panther ghost?" she asked. "I don't get it. What does an old legend have to do with staying away from the bonfire?"

"It's not just an old legend." Tisha leaned forward, her eyes bright. "People have seen him up there, Holly. They've seen the Los Gatos Panther."

"Not for years!" Jason waved away her words with one hand.

"That's not true." Tisha glanced over her shoulder and lowered her voice. "There's an old guy who comes into my grandmother's store. He says he saw it. And that was last month. And don't forget Brady McIntyre."

Jason tipped his chair so that it rested on the two back legs. "Brady McIntyre was a crazy old man."

"Yeah, a crazy old man they found dead." Tisha wasn't about to let Jason dismiss her fears so easily. She crinkled her nose at him. "When they found him," she told Holly, "what they found of him, they said it looked like he'd been mauled by a cat."

"Rumors!" Jason dropped his chair back into its proper place and reached for the pile of cookies in his lunchbag. He downed them along with his last carton of milk.

"People are always looking for thrills," he said, wiping cookie crumbs from his face with the back of his hand. "They're willing to believe anything if it supports some dumb old spooky legend. Me? I don't believe a word of it. I believe just what the police said. Brady was lost in the woods. You know how confused he could get sometimes. He was stumbling through the woods and he fell over a ledge. End of story."

Tisha sat up, her shoulders squared. "And what about the pawprints people have seen?"

"What about them?" Jason sat up straight, too. A dark flush stained his cheeks. "I'd say they're about as real as the Bigfoot tracks some folks claim to have seen and—"

Holly didn't give Jason a chance to get any further. "Wait a minute, you two." She interrupted with the only question she could think of that might at least begin to stop their bickering. "Just tell me something. All this panther stuff, is that why the town's called Los Gatos?"

Jason snapped his mouth closed. He obviously loved a good debate and he looked disappointed when he realized this one was at an end. "Nah," he said. "The Spanish were the first to sight the Oregon coast. Back in the 1500s. There were lots of mountain lions in the area then, so they gave the place its name. Los Gatos. It means 'The Cats.' "

"Then why can't the footprints that people have found be from mountain lions?" Holly looked from Jason to Tisha, daring them to challenge the logic of her argument.

"Because no one's seen a mountain lion this close to Portland in years," Tisha began. "But they have seen the panther—"

"Because there aren't any cats to see. At all," Jason butted in. "No mountain lions. No panthers."

Holly threw her hands up in a gesture of surrender. These two were absolutely determined to argue, and there was probably only one way to stop it.

Hoping she didn't look nearly as ridiculous as she felt, she batted her eyes at Jason. "And what time will you pick me up next Thursday?" she asked.

"Gosh . . . yeah . . . Thursday." Reminding Jason about homecoming was enough to make him forget all about the legend. The color in his cheeks faded from bright red to a slightly embarrassed and kind of cute pink.

"Ah . . . I'll pick you up at eight-fifteen, I guess. And Saturday for the dance . . ." Jason's eyes widened. He hopped out of his chair. "The dance! I almost forgot!" He grabbed his books from the table and was already out the cafeteria door when they heard his voice trailing down the hallway. "I've got to call my mom. She'll have to get my sportcoat cleaned."

Holly laughed. She was still laughing when she heard a voice just behind her.

"His sportcoat. Isn't that sweet!"

Holly's laugh evaporated. She spun in her chair. Laila Sarandon was standing not too far away and she'd obviously overheard everything they were talking about. She tossed a look from the cafeteria door to the group of girls who hovered around her like bees around a bunch of flowers. "Hasn't anybody told that guy you're supposed to wear a suit to homecoming? What a loser!"

Her comment was met with giggles, the loudest from Amber and Lindsey who were right beside Laila.

Before Holly could even think of anything to say, Tisha was out of her chair. "That's not fair, Laila," Tisha said. "You know Jason probably doesn't even own a suit. His folks don't have much money and—"

Laila didn't give Tisha a chance to finish. She laughed, the sound light and airy and so full of contempt it made Holly's blood run cold.

By this time, just about everyone left in the cafeteria had gathered in a loose circle around the girls. Realizing she was attracting a crowd, Laila flicked her mane of shiny black hair over her shoulder. Her eyes gleamed with satisfaction. Jason had told Holly that Laila was the star of the drama club and right now, Holly could believe it. Laila had her audience in the palm of her hand, waiting on her every word, and she used their interest to her best advantage.

She cast a glance around the circle of curious onlookers and lifted her shoulders in the kind of gesture that clearly said she was being forced to speak the truth, whether she wanted to or not. "Maybe Jason could afford better clothes," Laila said with a sigh, "if his dad didn't drink away every penny they had. Sad but true. And if he can't dress right, he ought to just stay home."

"It's not the people who can't afford to dress right who should stay home. It's the people who don't have any manners."

Holly was nearly as surprised to hear her own voice as she was to learn all this about Jason. It was all news to her, the fact that Jason couldn't afford a suit for homecoming, the fact that his dad was a drinker. It was all news. And it didn't matter one bit.

She wasn't sorry for what she'd said to Laila, especially when she watched the smug expression on Laila's face fade into a look of absolute astonishment.

Holly laughed.

This felt good, really good, and she rubbed her thumbs over the tips of her fingers, savoring the feeling of excitement that vibrated through her veins.

It felt good to stand up to Laila after suffering weeks of her withering looks. It felt good to see her surprise, to watch her astonishment as she realized there was someone—anyone—who was willing to confront her. It felt good to be angry. Very good.

Holly looked over to Tisha to see if she was enjoying the show.

Tisha's face had gone pale, her eyes were wide and as round as almond-shaped eyes were ever likely to get. She motioned Holly with one hand, the gesture clearly designed as one of warning.

Holly ignored her. She ignored Amber and Lindsey standing behind Laila like well-dressed bodyguards. She even ignored Alex. Holly could just see his dark head through the crowd. He hadn't gotten up from his seat, but she could tell he was watching. She could feel his eyes on her.

She didn't care.

Holly drew in a deep breath and rose from her chair.

She and Laila were about the same height, and Holly looked the other girl up and down before she looked her straight in the eyes. For a moment, it was all she could do.

There was something about the look in Laila's eyes that snatched Holly's breath out of her lungs and caused her heart to throb painfully against her ribs. Something old and so beautiful Holly did not want to look away. Something so terrifying, she could not turn away if she tried.

"No one can do this to me and get away with it."

It was as if she heard Laila's voice, but Holly knew it wasn't possible. Laila hadn't moved. She hadn't spoken. She had simply returned Holly's contemptuous look with one of her own.

"Back off. Now. While you can."

These were not Laila's words. For the briefest of moments, Holly let her gaze flicker to Tisha. Is this where the warning was coming from?

No. Tisha looked too upset to warn anyone about anything.

"Back off."

Like an alarm, the words rang through Holly's head. She wasn't sure where they came from, but she knew it would be wise to follow the advice. Laila Sarandon was not someone to challenge. She should back off.

But she didn't.

Holly took a step forward until the toes of her tennis shoes were just touching the tips of Laila's expensive leather flats.

"I said, it's not the people who can't afford to dress right who should stay home." Holly repeated the words, not because she didn't think Laila had heard them, but to make sure everyone else in the crowd had. "It's the people who don't have any manners who ought to be kept off the streets."

Laila sucked in a tiny breath of surprise. "I can't imagine what you're talking about," she said.

"Oh? Then let me explain." No one could have been more surprised than Holly at how smooth and composed she sounded. "What I mean is that people who make fun of other people are about the lowest form of life around. Like the flatworms we were talking about in biology today. I'll bet even a flatworm wouldn't make fun of a perfectly nice guy just 'cause his parents don't have much money and his dad has a drinking problem."

In a perfect imitation of Laila's snobbish gesture, Holly tossed her hair over her shoulder. She laughed and tried to make the sound as snobbish as the one she had heard Laila use to such devastating effect.

It obviously worked. Laila looked furious. And that made Holly feel twice as daring. She glanced at the crowd, then pinned Laila with a look. "What a shame," she said, "to be outclassed by a flatworm!"

She didn't wait to see Laila's reaction.

Holly spun on her heels, grabbed Tisha's arm and was out of the cafeteria door in record time.

Without stopping, she dragged Tisha through the first floor hallway, up the stairs, all the way to the third floor and the school library.

She dropped into the first empty chair she saw.

Tisha collapsed into the chair across from Holly's. She looked like a fish that had just been hooked and brought onto shore. Her mouth opened. It closed. It opened again.

"You're crazy!" Tisha's voice sounded like a croak.

It was all she could say for a long time. She simply sat there, staring at Holly and, after a minute, she smiled, a tiny smile that brightened her eyes and pushed her cheeks up until they looked like shiny apples.

"You're crazy!" she said again. Her smile turned into a full-fledged, ear-to-ear grin. "No one has ever talked to Laila that way. It's about time someone put her in her place. You were great! You were better than great. You were awesome!"

"Yeah." Now that the whole thing was over, Holly thought she knew exactly how boxers felt after they were hit square in the stomach. She pressed one hand to her heart and fought to catch her breath.

"Awesome," she said, repeating the word, as amazed by her own courage as Tisha was.

But, Holly wondered, if she was so awesome, why were her hands shaking?

Red hair.

Red hair and freckles scattered across her face like a sprinkle of cinnamon.

Alex Sarandon sat back in his chair and crossed his arms over his chest.

Before now, he hadn't noticed just how red her hair was.

It glimmered in the light of the overhead fluorescents, red like copper, its shining strands catching the light and throwing it back in gold and crimson highlights.

Red like a sunset. Strands of it red as blood.

Alex felt a tingle in his mouth, like the prickle that comes from eating something sour. He ran his tongue over his lips, banishing the craving.

He braced his broad shoulders against the back of his chair and stuck his long legs out in front of him. He wasn't listening to anything Laila and Holly were saying.

It didn't matter.

He hadn't had this much fun in ages.

Finally, there was someone who actually had the guts to stand up to Laila.

Alex felt a grin tickle the corners of his mouth.

It was enough to make his day.

Someone was actually strong enough—or crazy enough—to put his sister in her place.

Someone with red hair.

Alex watched Holly deliver what was obviously some stinging remark. She didn't wait around to hear Laila's reply and he didn't blame her. Laila was about to burst like an old steam pipe.

But Holly didn't give her a chance.

She spun around and headed out the door, her coppery hair flowing behind her like a stream of molten lava.

Alex felt his grin lift into a smile, his smile turn into a chuckle. He didn't stop laughing, not even when

Laila turned on him, fire in her eyes.

"You could have come to my defense." Laila snatched her books from the table and glared down at him. "You could have said something to the little brat."

But Alex didn't say anything at all. He couldn't stop laughing.

This was going to be interesting, he told himself. The awareness made his blood sing in his veins.

This was going to be very interesting.

4

"Absolutely. Positively. Not."

Tisha glared at Holly. Her mouth was screwed into a frown, her eyes were squinched, as if the color of Holly's hair, more red than ever in the light of the setting sun, was too dazzling.

"I am not going to the bonfire. And I wish you wouldn't, either."

Like a turtle retreating into its shell, Tisha stepped back into the house. Holly was certain she would have slammed the front door in her face if Holly's foot wasn't firmly wedged in it.

Time to regroup.

Holly took a deep breath and considered her options. It didn't take long. There didn't seem to be any options, short of kidnapping Tisha and spiriting her off to the bonfire. Holly had already tried every other enticement she could think of.

There was the promise of hot new gossip—the homecoming bonfire was traditionally the place to check out who was dating who that year.

That hadn't worked. Probably, Holly suspected, because Tisha already knew who was dating who.

There was Zack Wright waiting with Jason out in the car.

That one hadn't worked either. Tisha knew she'd see Zack the next day at the homecoming game. And Saturday at the dance.

There was only one other thing Holly could think to try.

She gave Tisha a soulful look, trying her best to look miserable at the same time she hoped she wasn't overplaying the part and turning off Tisha completely. "You've got to come," Holly said. "It's my very first homecoming. My very first bonfire. How can I have any fun without my best friend?"

Tisha rolled her eyes and clicked her tongue. She looked almost as annoyed with Holly as she did with herself. "I'll get my coat." Tisha hadn't gone two steps when she spun back around. "What are you wearing?" she asked.

"My good black jeans." Holly unbuttoned her jacket far enough for Tisha to see the collar of her shirt. "And my mom let me borrow her Irish knit sweater. I've got it over one of my dad's striped dress shirts."

"Give me a minute." Tisha still didn't look happy, but at least she was moving.

Holly gave the boys in the car the thumbs-up and stood back to wait.

In less than a minute, Tisha was back. She had added a heavy, hooded sweatshirt to her outfit, blue jeans and a bulky flannel shirt. There were three pairs of shoes lined up by the front door. Tisha slipped into a pair of moccasins.

"We're going to have a great time!" Before Tisha could change her mind, Holly threaded one arm through hers and tugged her toward the car.

But Tisha wasn't ready to leave. Not yet. She planted her feet and unwound herself from Holly's grip. She propped her fists on her hips.

"Promise me," Tisha said. There wasn't a bit of amusement in her expression. She looked as solemn as someone going to a funeral. "Promise me you won't wander away from the crowd."

Holly laughed and started toward the car. "Why would I?"

"I mean it, Holly." Tisha was more serious than ever. "Promise me you and Jason won't sneak off somewhere to be alone—"

"Tisha!" Holly felt her cheeks get hot. Being alone with Jason was the furthest thing from her mind. She didn't have a chance to tell Tisha, though. Tisha continued as if she hadn't heard Holly's protest.

"Promise me you won't leave the bonfire for any reason. Any reason."

It wasn't that Holly didn't appreciate Tisha's concern, but this was getting ridiculous. She threw her hands in the air. "Not even if a hungry bear comes running out of the woods and heads straight for me?"

Tisha didn't smile. "Not even for hungry bears," she said.

"Not even if a UFO beams me aboard?"

"Not for UFOs."

"Not even if the Los Gatos Panther shows up and carries me off?" The second the words were past her lips, Holly knew it was the wrong thing to say.

Tisha's face went pale. "It isn't funny!" She stamped

her foot. "Look, Holly, I know you think I'm nuts. I know you think it's all a big joke. But listen to me, will you? It isn't funny and it isn't a joke. I know what my grandmother has told me. And I've heard what other people have said about Panther Hollow. It's not smart to go wandering around there alone. Especially at night. I'm not so worried about me. I may be a chicken, but that means I'm not going to do anything stupid. It's your attitude that worries me. I'm not stepping off this front porch until you promise me that you're not going to leave the bonfire."

"All right." Holly felt guilty for making fun of what Tisha took so seriously. "I'm sorry," she said.

"And?" Tisha waited for more.

"And I promise." Feeling more than a little foolish, Holly crossed her heart with one finger. "I promise I will not leave the crowd," she said. "I swear I will not go wandering around Panther Hollow alone. Or with Jason. Or with anyone else. I won't go anywhere near Harper's Mountain alone. There. I hope you're satisfied. You don't have to be afraid anymore."

"You just don't get it, do you?" Tisha shook her head. She didn't look annoyed, she just looked frustrated and a little upset. "I'm not scared for me," she said. "I don't know why, Holly. I can't explain it. But I'm scared for you."

Panther Hollow gave her the creeps.

Holly pulled the collar of her blue jacket closer to her neck and looked around.

The Hollow was a flat, grassy area at the very top

of the high, steep hill everyone in Los Gatos called Harper's Mountain.

She wasn't very good at guessing distances, but Holly could tell the Hollow was big. It seemed to stretch out forever, its farthest edges cloaked in darkness and ringed with a circle of trees that looked purple in the twilight.

She and Jason were walking toward the center of the Hollow where some kids were busy positioning fallen logs in a large semicircle. At the heart of the circle, other kids were piling twigs and branches for the homecoming bonfire.

From what Jason had explained on the way over, Holly knew that it was a Los Gatos tradition to hold the bonfire here. As to why the place was called Panther Hollow . . . well, he said that was a tradition, too, and she'd find out more about it before the night was over.

Holly watched the sky above her head deepen from sapphire blue to navy and a nervous little quiver squirmed up her back. Hoping to make the feeling go away, she twitched her shoulders. It didn't help. One more look around Panther Hollow confirmed her original impression.

The place gave her the cold creeps.

Maybe it was the last flickers of sunshine that skimmed the horizon and sent long dark shadows across the ground like skeleton fingers. Maybe it was the melancholy call of an owl that sounded clear and lonely above the noises of the crowd. Maybe it was the place itself.

Whatever it was, Holly was certain of one thing. She never had to make that promise to Tisha back at the house. She wasn't about to go wandering around Panther Hollow alone.

Zack and Tisha were walking up ahead and Holly squinted past them into the gathering darkness. Along the edges of the Hollow, she could just make out the ruins of long, low buildings, piles of bricks and broken chimneys and fallen roofs sticking out of the ground like dinosaur bones.

"What is this place?" Holly pulled to a stop. Her voice was no louder than the wind that whispered through the long grass.

Jason was walking at her side. He stopped, too, and looked at her as if she'd just started speaking Russian. "It's Panther Hollow."

"I know that." Holly gave him a tight smile. "I mean all this." She swept one arm toward the ruined buildings.

"I keep forgetting you're new to Los Gatos." Jason didn't seemed nearly as moved by the atmosphere of the place as Holly was. He grabbed her hand and dragged her toward the bonfire circle, talking as they went. "It's the old camp," he said.

"Camp?" There was something sinister about the word. Holly felt goosebumps tickle their way down her arms.

From up ahead Tisha heard them talking. She waited until they caught up. As usual, she was left to explain what Jason didn't feel like talking about. "It was an internment camp," Tisha said. "One of the places where Japanese-Americans were held during World War II."

Holly shivered. "Doesn't it bother you?"

"The camp?" Tisha paused as if she'd never considered the question before. "Sure it does," she finally admitted, a little too casually to mask her true feelings. "I guess that could be one of the reasons I hate this place so much. I've heard so many stories about it from Grammy—"

"Was she—?" The words stuck in Holly's throat.

"Here? During the war? Sure." Tisha tossed off the words, but her face suddenly looked years older and wiser. "She stayed in Los Gatos after the war was over. Said she got to like the place."

"There's dozens of ruined buildings all through these woods," Jason broke in. Either he was unaware of how upset Tisha was or he was hoping to steer the conversation in another direction. Holly suspected he was trying to spare Tisha's feelings and the thought caused a delicious warmth to spread in her stomach.

"The place is a nightmare for the police department," Jason continued. "Kind of a combination drinking hangout and lovers' lane."

The last words faded on Jason's lips at the same time a fierce rush of color stained his cheeks. He cleared his throat and looked away. "It's one of the reasons our parents don't like us hanging around here any night but tonight."

"One of the reasons." Tisha gave him a meaningful look.

Jason obviously was not going to let Tisha bring up

anything to do with ghosts. He was holding Holly's hand and before Tisha could say anything else, he wound his fingers through Holly's and sprinted toward the logs that were placed around the bonfire as seats.

He found an empty log at the front and slipped into a seat next to Ben Wiley and his date. Holly sat beside him. Tisha was on her left. Zack was next to Tisha. Holly didn't understand how they'd gotten here so late and still been able to get seats in the first row. She was about to ask Jason when Mr. Peters, the school principal, walked to the center of the circle.

The homecoming ceremony was about to start.

Mr. Peters cleared his throat and looked around. When he was certain he had everyone's attention, he began.

"Each year," he said, "we come together to celebrate the beginning of a new school year and to cheer our Los Gatos Panthers on to another successful football season!"

The crowd cheered.

"This year is no different," he continued. "This year . . ."

Mr. Peters launched into a talk about school spirit, and sportsmanship, and the Panthers' chance of making the state playoffs. His speech was short on excitement, long on words, and the more he talked, the more Holly found her attention wandering.

She let her gaze stray to the girls who were stationed at the edges of the crowd, flaming torches held high above their heads.

Tisha poked Holly in the ribs with her elbow. She

was apparently bored, too. She was watching as Holly looked around. "Cheerleaders," she whispered in Holly's ear.

Holly could see that. They were wearing short black skirts and white sweaters with a black panther embroidered across the front.

Amber and Lindsey were there, along with a couple of girls Holly didn't recognize. At the front of the pack was Laila Sarandon.

She looked fabulous in the firelight. Holly watched Laila and a prick of jealousy gnawed at her insides.

She wondered what it would be like to be as cool and sophisticated as Laila, to have sleek black hair instead of silly red, to have cheekbones that looked like they were sculpted and eyes that were as mysterious and fascinating as a cat's.

She wondered what it would be like to know Alex as well as Laila did.

Holly slapped the thought away. She felt like a traitor, sitting here next to Jason, thinking about Alex.

Still, she couldn't help herself. She glanced around the bonfire circle and wondered where Alex was tonight.

It didn't take long to find out.

Mr. Peters finished his speech and the crowd applauded politely. When the clapping died down, Stan Buckowski, the football coach, stepped up to the front.

The coach had been affectionately dubbed Bucky by LGH students and it was clear he was one of the crowd's favorites. Their respectful applause turned into cheers. The cheering got louder and louder until it echoed around Harper's Mountain like thunder and Bucky had to wave his hands and ask for silence. Once he got it, he didn't waste any time. He introduced this year's LGH Panthers.

Along with the rest of the crowd, Holly cheered. They cheered for the junior varsity team and for the cheerleaders. They cheered for the second-string players and for the seniors who would be playing their last season this year. Finally, they cheered for the team's leaders.

As co-captain and quarterback, Alex was the last to come out. If Holly thought Laila looked fabulous in the firelight she was certain Alex looked better than fabulous. He was wearing his white football jersey over dark jeans. His hair was blacker than the sky above their heads, his eyes sparkled in the light of the torches. He stood on Bucky's right, hands behind his back, the fitful light of the torches throwing restless shadows that caressed his broad shoulders one moment and stroked his jaw with darkness the next.

His gaze traveled over the crowd and Holly was certain it stopped on her.

Not that she saw it. By this time, it was hard to see anything. Everyone was on their feet cheering.

But she felt it.

She felt Alex's eyes. They were cool against the hot flush that invaded her cheeks. They were hot against the ice that settled in her stomach.

They were on her.

And gone again so quickly, Holly shook herself like a person coming out of a hypnotic trance and wondered if her imagination wasn't working overtime.

She jumped when Jason touched her arm.

"This is the best part." Jason's face was bright and eager in the light of the torches. He pointed to the cheerleaders. They had come to the front of the crowd and were standing around the bonfire pile, torches raised.

On Bucky's count of three, the cheerleaders stabbed their torches into the woodpile. A deafening cheer echoed across Panther Hollow as the branches caught and flamed.

The bonfire was enormous. Holly tipped her head back and watched the flames shoot to the sky, their brightness overpowering the far-off sparkle of the stars.

The fire's light encased the Hollow in a soft, orange glow. Holly twirled around to see it surrounding them. It was as if they'd all been trapped in one of those glass water balls that her mother collected. The ones with the fake snow inside that floated when the ball was turned over. All color and magic inside, darkness and cold outside.

Though she tried not to, Holly found herself staring at the edge of the Hollow, out where the fire's light could not penetrate the darkness of the woods beyond or warm whatever might be in them.

She was still staring when Jason nudged her.

"This is our big moment," he said.

Holly didn't ask what he was talking about. The

last of the applause was fading and Alex was nowhere to be seen. Along with the rest of the crowd, Holly dropped back into her seat.

No sooner did the crowd quiet down than Ben Wiley rose to his feet. He headed to the front of the circle.

Ben stopped right in front of the bonfire and gave the crowd the kind of look Holly had seen kids give their dentists. Ben's eyes were wide, his hands were shaking. He shrugged his shoulders in his jacket, shifted his weight from foot to foot, and smoothed out a piece of paper he had clutched in his hands.

"Each year at homecoming," Ben read from the paper, "it's an LGH junior class tradition to retell the story of the Los Gatos Panther. This year . . ." Ben made the mistake of looking up from the paper. He promptly lost his place. His ears turned scarlet and he quietly read through the first part of his speech until he found where he'd left off.

"This year," Ben said again, "the members of the junior class would like to do something a little different. The homecoming committee, under the direction of Jason Van Kirk, has written its own version of the Panther legend. We'd like to share that story with you. We'll start with . . ." Ben turned the sheet of paper over in his hands. "We'll start with Laila Sarandon."

The introduction was met with a smattering of applause.

Laila stepped forward.

Holly had to give her credit, the girl could look as good as the best of them. Her face was flushed with excitement and firelight. Her posture was perfect. Her voice, when she raised it and spoke, was composed and confident.

"The story of the Los Gatos Panther begins back in 1882," Laila said. Unlike Ben, she wasn't reading her lines from a piece of paper. She had them memorized and she was looking at the crowd, a smile on her face, obviously enjoying being the center of attention.

"Back then, Los Gatos was nothing more than a logging town, a small village surrounded by untamed wilderness. Historical records tell us that there was a general store where McBride's Restaurant now stands. There was a church, a town hall, a barbershop that doubled as a dentist's office. The people of Los Gatos worked long and hard. There wasn't much entertainment available to them. Except when the circus came to town."

It was Zack's turn to continue the story. He slid out of his seat next to Tisha and walked to the front.

"It was a small circus that came to town that um . . . that spring," he said, staring straight ahead of himself. "There was a family of acrobats, a . . . um, a magician, and a clown. There was also an animal trainer. The man's name was George Ensor. At least that's what's recorded in the town history. George had two trained brown bears, a seal that could play the horns and balance a ball on the end of its nose . . . and a black panther."

At that moment, a gust of wind wailed over the Hollow. The bonfire hopped and wavered, sending wild shadows dancing over the crowd. Zack's eyes got big, as if he expected to see the Los Gatos Panther himself leap out of the crowd.

"Pretty good special effects, huh?" Jason didn't look nearly as rattled as Zack did. He nodded his approval and glanced around at the startled expressions on the faces of those around them. "That couldn't have been more perfect if it was planned. Maybe I should be in charge of this thing every year." He paused, considering the idea. "Maybe I could get a real panther to . . ." The cheerful expression faded from Jason's face when he looked over and saw that Tisha was about to bolt out of her seat.

"Hey, Little Bit, I was only kidding." Jason reached over Holly and patted Tisha's arm. "You aren't scared, are you?" He didn't wait for an answer. He wrapped one arm around Holly's shoulders and Holly wound her arm through Tisha's.

By this time, the fire had settled down and Amber had come forward to continue the story.

She looked as bored as Holly had seen her look in Math class. Amber tossed her long blonde hair over one shoulder and rolled her eyes. "The circus stayed in town for . . . for like a week and people came from, like, all over to see it," she said. "According to the newspapers of the day, everyone had a . . . like, a swell time."

Jason cringed. "That's the last time I'll give her a part in one of my extravaganzas," he grumbled.

Holly silenced him with a look. She wanted to hear the rest of the story.

"There was a circus performance almost every day,"

Amber said. "Two on Saturday. None on Sunday.
And George Ensor took advantage of that Sunday to,
like . . . relax."

Amber stepped back. Jason slid his arm from Holly's shoulders and stood.

He was trying not to look nervous, but Holly could
tell he was. He was talking before he ever got as far
as the front of the circle.

"George was quite a guy, from all the records that
have survived," Jason said, glancing at the crowd.
"He was quite the ladies' man. He spent all of that
Sunday courting the Widow Riley who lived up on
Pine Ridge. He didn't get back until late Sunday night.
And when he did, he found that his prized panther was
missing."

Jason was a pretty good actor. He paused and let
the significance of the statement sink in before he
continued.

"Gone," Jason said with a shrug. "The town searched
high and low, but there was even more wilderness here
then. There wasn't much chance they were going to
find that panther. After a week or so, they stopped
trying. The circus moved on and the people of Los
Gatos figured they wouldn't have to worry about the
panther once winter came. No tropical animal could
survive an Oregon winter. People forgot about the
panther. Until the next summer."

Jason stepped back and a girl in a pretty pink jacket
took his place.

"The next summer," she said, "Madelaine and
Robert Marchmount went out to have a picnic.

They were brother and sister, twins, and they were the only children of Dr. Richard Marchmount, one of Los Gatos's leading citizens. No one thought a thing of it. People had been picnicking here on Harper's Mountain for as long as anyone could remember. No one worried about the twins until they didn't come back from that picnic."

"Until they were found dead." This was Alex's voice and it caused Holly to jump in her seat. He was somewhere behind her, but she didn't dare turn around to see where. Instead, Holly watched the aisle next to where they sat, waiting for him to come into view.

She didn't have to wait long.

His shoulders squared, his head high, Alex walked slowly toward the front of the audience, telling his part of the story in a voice that was as icy as the shadows beyond the fire.

"Their throats were torn open." Alex arrived at the front of the crowd and swung around to face them. Punctuated by the crackle of the fire, his words fell like stones.

The raging fire had made Laila look beautiful. It had made Jason look as comfortable as a tabby cat asleep in front of a fireplace. It made Alex look more mysterious than ever. The fire rose up behind him like a halo, outlining his body with flame.

Holly fastened her eyes on him, unable to look away, her fascination with him and the story he was telling so complete, she would have sworn he was telling the story to her. Only to her.

"The Marchmount twins were torn to pieces by what could only have been a cat," Alex said. "It couldn't have been one of the mountain lions who lived in the region. No mountain lion kills the way a panther does. You see, the panther is a selfish animal." He paused for the briefest of heartbeats and looked at his sister.

"The panther doesn't like to share with others. That's why it drags its kill up into the branches of a convenient tree. And that's where they found the Marchmount twins. Their bodies hidden in the branches of a tree, twenty feet off the ground. Their throats torn open."

Though Alex's words were powerful, his voice was soft, hypnotic. The story filled Holly with disgust at the same time it caused a purr of excitement to curl through her. It made her knees weak and her hands tremble, and she pulled her arm away from Tisha's before Tisha could feel it, too.

Alex stepped back into the shadows and Ben Wiley came forward again. "Everyone said it couldn't be George Ensor's panther," Ben said. He had lowered his voice and was trying his best to sound spooky. The effect would have been far scarier if Ben wasn't reading his lines.

"But no other animal kills like a panther. No other animal is as strong. Or as cunning, or as clever. That's why we honor the Los Gatos Panther here tonight. The panther"— Ben looked around —"was never found. But his ghostly shape can still be seen on moonless nights here in Panther Hollow."

Ben looked to his right. He looked to his left. Holly

found herself looking around, too, in spite of the fact that she felt foolish doing it.

Tisha wasn't looking around, Holly noticed. She was hunched over on her end of the log, arms crossed over her chest, head down, eyes squeezed closed.

"And in honor of the Panther," Ben went on, his voice rising, "we're going to trounce John Kennedy High in the game tomorrow!"

The spell of the Panther myth was broken. Everyone jumped to their feet and cheered. Everyone except Tisha.

Holly clapped only long enough to show her support. As soon as she could, she sat back down.

"It's over now." She bent and tilted her head to try to attract Tisha's attention.

Tisha's eyes were still closed.

Holly tried again. "They're done with the story."

"Are they?" Tisha opened her eyes slowly, like a person waking from a nightmare, afraid that the dream might turn out to be real. "I was trying not to listen."

"It's just a dumb old story." Zack must have been talking to Jason about the legend: He sounded just as cynical about it as Jason did. He had waded his way back through the crowd and was standing looking down at them. He reached one hand down for Tisha's and pulled her to her feet. "It was just for fun, Tish. Let's forget about that crazy legend and get some cider," he said. He tugged Tisha into the crowd.

Jason was behind him. "Well," he asked, "what did you think?"

"I liked it." Holly hopped to her feet. She wasn't lying. She did enjoy the program, and she was happy to finally find out what the panther legend was all about. But she didn't dare tell Jason what the story had done to her insides. Her head still felt dizzy, her heart raced like a speedboat. She hid her reaction behind a smile. "Did you write it?"

Jason blushed. "Some of it," he confessed. He looked pleased to have Holly's approval. "It was pretty good, wasn't it?"

Holly laughed and threaded her arm through his. "It was better than good," she said, hoping her apprehension didn't show in her voice. "It was great. Now can we get some cider?"

Jason nodded his consent and pulled her into the crowd. The refreshment stands were set up along the far edge of the Hollow and everyone seemed to be headed that way. It was pretty obvious they wouldn't be able to walk side-by-side for long. Jason grabbed Holly's hand.

"Stay close!" He yelled to her over the noises of the crowd.

That was next to impossible. Someone jostled Holly from behind and she let go of Jason's hand.

"You go on ahead!" She called to him and waved him toward the refreshment stands. "I'll meet you up there."

Jason nodded his agreement.

It was getting harder and harder to move. Holly had the sudden feeling of being trapped. Her heart pounded. Her breathing was tight and painful. She was being pressed on every side and she needed to get out.

There was a stack of bricks piled just at the border where the clearing met the tall trees. Holly weaved her way to it, her heart still beating like the bass section of a heavy-metal song. She would wait here until the crowd thinned, she decided, and meet Jason in a few minutes.

Holly perched on the edge of the bricks and gulped in a long breath of crisp night air.

Out here away from the bonfire, the air seemed colder, the shadows dark and brittle.

She hunched her shoulders against the cold and looked back toward the refreshment stands. The crowd had thinned a little, it was time to meet Jason.

"Holly!"

Holly sat up. She could have sworn she heard some-one calling her name from inside the woods.

That was impossible.

She shook away the thought and concentrated on watching the assortment of people who were scuffling around the Hollow.

"Holly!"

She heard the voice again.

Or did she?

As if her brain were a tape recorder and she could simply hit the rewind button, Holly tried to replay the sound.

It wasn't so much a voice, she decided, thinking it over. It wasn't even so much a sound she heard. It was more like a vibration, a tremor just on the edges of her consciousness, something that pricked her to attention and summoned her.

Holly spun in her seat and peered into the woods.

"Holly! Please!" The voice sounded louder this time. It sounded frightened.

"You've got to help me. I'm—"

The sound faded away on a sob that rose to the trees and disappeared into the blackness beyond the stars.

Holly bolted from her seat. This time, there was no mistaking it. There was a voice in the woods. A voice calling to her.

She was certain of it now.

Just as she was certain she knew who was calling for help.

It was Tisha.

—— 5 ——

Her lungs felt like they were on fire.

Holly braced herself against the nearest tree.

Each time she inhaled, the cool night air stabbed her insides. Each time she exhaled, she was sure she would never have the strength to draw another breath.

Propping her hands on her knees, she bent over and ordered herself to slow down.

"One. Two. Three."

She pulled in a painful breath, measuring out the counts to force herself to concentrate, just like she did when she was running the track.

"One. Two. Three."

She held the breath until it felt like her lungs would burst.

"One. Two. Three."

She let it out again.

She made herself repeat the exercise twice.

Finally, her heartbeat slowed, her breathing relaxed. It was only then she allowed herself to think.

Holly straightened and brushed the hair out of her eyes.

How long had she been running? How far had she come?

It couldn't be more than a few minutes, she told herself.

And in the dark, sidestepping tree roots and low-hanging branches and rabbit holes that showed suddenly in the ground at her feet, she couldn't have come more than a few hundred yards from the Hollow.

It felt more like a few million.

Holly glanced back over her shoulder.

At this time of year, the trees were still full of leaves. They lay like a dark canopy overhead, blotting out the sky, smothering the noise of the homecoming festivities until it sounded no more real than the half-remembered echoes of a dream.

The leaves high above her and the pine needles at her feet acted like insulation, deadening all sound, and Holly realized suddenly that she hadn't heard a thing since she'd entered the woods. Not the sound of night birds, or the scurrying of small animals. She hadn't even heard Tisha call to her again.

Though she was sure she hadn't felt a breeze, the leaves on the tree above Holly's head rattled. Startled, she looked up in time to see the branches twist and quiver. Beyond them, she could just see the smudge of the bonfire's flames lighting the sky with a glow as red as blood.

Holly's heartbeat may have slowed, but her imagination was working overtime. Thinking about blood didn't help.

She'd been too busy running to notice before, but now Holly realized her hands were trembling, her knees felt rubbery and weak. And not just from racing through the woods.

There was something out here she didn't like, though she couldn't put a name to it. Something—some Presence—that crept over her like an icy wind and seeped down inside her until her bones rattled and her blood ran cold and her skin felt as if it were too tight to hold her. Something that called to her as surely as Tisha had called her name.

Something she didn't want to meet.

Holly looked around.

Behind her the woods were dark and silent as a tomb. On either side of her, they spread off into endless blackness. In front of her, maybe twenty yards ahead, stood what was left of one of the camp buildings, its walls sagging, a tangle of vines snaking endlessly around the weathered wood boards. Its roof was collapsed at one end. Its windows were gone. Their empty frames stared back at Holly like the eye sockets of a skull.

A lump of terror shot up in Holly's throat.

What was Tisha doing out here anyway? And who was she with?

A series of terrifying images filled Holly's mind.

Zack Wright seemed like a nice enough guy, but how well did they really know him? Maybe he and Tisha had a fight? Maybe they'd argued? Maybe he shoved her? Hit her? Hurt her?

Holly pushed aside the thoughts as quickly as she could. It wasn't quick enough.

Her breathing picked up speed, until her head felt dizzy and the scene in front of her blurred. Her eyes filled with tears of anger and frustration.

Why had she been stupid enough to think she could find Tisha alone? Why had she been reckless enough to leave the Hollow without getting help first?

Help.

The word shimmered like a candle in the dark, sparking a flicker of hope in Holly's heart.

She would go back.

She would get help.

Holly spun around. She had already taken two steps back toward the Hollow when she heard something.

This time, it wasn't Tisha's voice. It wasn't any voice at all. It was a moan, a cry that sounded thin and brittle and so desolate, it made Holly forget her fears.

"Tisha!"

Holly spun back around. She was certain the cry came from the camp building. She broke into a run, calling Tisha's name.

Like the windows, the door of the old building was missing. Holly stood at the bottom of a set of rickety steps, staring into the gaping hole. It was black. Open. Empty. Like a newly dug grave.

Never taking her eyes off the doorway, Holly inched her way up the rotted stairs, testing each step cautiously before she put her full weight on it. At the top of the stairs, she stopped.

"Tisha?"

Her voice did not sound nearly as bold now as it did when she charged into the woods. It echoed back at Holly, a question that faded on the wind along with her hopes.

"Tisha?"

Only the sound of her own voice answered her in the dark.

Holly poked her head into the building. Because of the collapsed roof, it wasn't as dark inside as she expected. She could make out the shapes of the discarded beer cans that littered the floor like fallen leaves. She could see that in one corner there was a pile of fast food cartons, in another, what was left of the front seat of some old car.

"Tisha?" Holly's voice fell dead against the silence. Her hands out in front of her, she groped her way into the building, trying to make her voice sound braver than she felt. "Tisha. It's me, Holly. I'm here. Where are you? What's wrong? Tisha?"

There was no answer.

Holly looked around.

Of course there was no answer, she told herself. There was no one here.

Holly's shoulders sagged. She wasn't sure if she should feel relief or disappointment.

Instead, she just felt confused.

She whirled around, examining the ruined building one last time.

There was no sign that anyone had been here tonight. No place for a person to hide if they were there. No reason Tisha would not answer her now when she'd been calling for help all this time.

It was baffling.

Convinced she wouldn't find the answer here in this empty building, Holly turned around, ready to leave.

She was just in time to see a quick movement in the

darkness between her and the door, a shadow deeper than the shadows around it, a hint of movement that was as smooth and quiet as a whisper.

Holly froze in place. Her veins filled with ice water at the same time another, terrifying realization filled her brain.

Tisha wasn't here.

But something else was.

Holly wasn't alone.

"Where's Holly?"

Holding her steaming cup of cider with both hands, Tisha plunked down next to Jason on one of the benches set up near the refreshment stands.

"I don't know." Jason scratched one hand through his hair. He craned his neck to look around the Hollow. Seeing no sign of Holly, he drank down the last of his cider, and started in on hers before it could get cold. "I thought she might be with you. If she's not, I guess she must have found somebody else to talk to."

"I saw her sitting over there when we were getting our drinks." With a tip of his white cardboard cup, Zack indicated the fallen bricks that were stacked just at the edge of the woods.

Jason nodded. "Yeah. I saw her over there, too. But by the time I turned around again, she was gone."

"Gone? What do you mean, gone?" Tisha sat up, her back as straight as an arrow, her dark brows low over her eyes. She set her cup on the bench and gripped Jason's arm. "You mean you haven't seen her for ten minutes and you haven't even started to look for her?"

"What's to look for?" Jason shook off Tisha's hand. "Unless she's got talents we haven't learned about yet, I don't think she disappeared into thin air." He teased Tisha with a smile and a quirk of his eyebrows. "Unless the panther got her."

Tisha didn't like the sound of that at all. She bolted to her feet and paced back and forth in front of the bench, her hands working over each other. Her eyes as watchful as a hawk's, she darted a look at the sea of faces around them, as if she could make Holly appear simply by willing it.

When that didn't work, Tisha's chin wrinkled, her lips puckered. Her fists on her hips, she stopped in front of the boys. "All right," she said with a look that said it was everything but all right. "You guys sit here and make fun of the whole thing. I'll go find Holly myself."

Jason and Zack exchanged looks. Humor her, their silent glances seemed to say, or it's going to be one long, miserable weekend.

"Why don't I help you?" Zack had the most to lose, so he offered his assistance first. Crumpling his cup in one hand, he tossed it into the nearest trash can and grabbed Tisha's arm.

"Why don't I come along?" Jason sprang out of his seat and snatched Tisha's other arm. "We'll go examine the scene of the crime," he said, steering them toward the pile of bricks. "Maybe we'll find a clue."

Tisha mumbled something that sounded pretty rude. Jason didn't press his luck. He kept his mouth shut and they started toward the spot where Holly had gone to wait.

It was almost as hard getting back there as it had been to get over to the refreshment stands. A bunch of students was jammed in a circle not far from the bonfire and the crowd was blocking their way.

"Something's up." Jason tugged Tisha and Zack to the edge of the crowd. He was the tallest of the three, and he stood on tiptoe and stretched to try to see over everyone's heads.

"It's Mr. Tollifson," he called back to Tisha and Zack. "He's got some sort of contraption he's showing off. Something that looks like a great big dog cage."

Jason settled back on his feet just before he was jostled by the kids who were already gathering behind them. One hand on Tisha's shoulder, he steadied himself and pulled her headlong into the crowd. "Come on," he said. "Everybody's here. This has got to be where Holly is."

It might have been because Jason was so tall. He moved through the crowd like a steamship through a group of pleasure boats.

It might have been because Zack was so polite. He excused himself every five seconds.

It might have been because Tisha was used to being the shortest person in any crowd and knew how to use her elbows to the best advantage.

Whatever the reason, the crowd parted before them. They got to the front just in time to hear Laila's voice, dripping with contempt.

"It's the most ridiculous thing I've ever heard!"

"Ridiculous? Why?" Mr. Tollifson spun to face Laila who was standing just to the right of Jason. Raising himself on the balls of his feet, he fixed Laila with his best Teacher Look and cleared his throat.

"The word 'ridiculous' is not applicable in scientific situations, Ms. Sarandon," he said. "Nothing in science is ridiculous. It simply is. Or it isn't. This panther everyone talks about isn't. Mass hysteria. That's what it is." As if he smelled something nasty, Mr. Tollifson sniffed.

"It's about time someone used some logical, rational methodology to disprove the whole thing," he said. "It's a legend. Nothing more. And I intend to demonstrate that before the school year's out."

Jason had never seen Laila interested in anything more academic than who was wearing what to the next dance. But something about Mr. Tollifson's plan seemed to have gotten her worked up. She took one step forward and settled her weight against her back foot.

"Why?" she demanded.

If Mr. Tollifson was as surprised as everyone else by Laila's sudden interest in science, he didn't show it. With a beaming smile, he welcomed the chance to continue his lecture.

"Why?" Mr. Tollifson pivoted around to take in the crowd. "Because I am a man of science. That's why. And this is an opportunity to involve my biology students in a study that is systematic and purposeful. We'll analyze feeding habits, migratory pat-

terns, environmental factors. We will bait the trap."
Mr. Tollifson made a dramatic gesture toward the
cage. "We will check it periodically. We will keep
clear, accurate records of everything that's caught."
He raised his eyebrows and looked directly at Laila.
"And everything that isn't."

"All in the name of science?" Laila still wasn't
ready to give up. She crossed her arms over her chest.

"All in the name of science." Mr. Tollifson snorted.
"I am certainly not interested in the supernatural if
that's what you're implying, Ms. Sarandon. And I
assure you, though we set our trap here in what is so
quaintly called Panther Hollow, we will never catch
anything more exotic than raccoons."

"Or skunks!" somebody called from the back of the
crowd.

Everyone laughed, including Mr. Tollifson. "Just
be careful when you're out here partying," he warned
with a shake of one pudgy finger. "I'd hate to find I've
caught myself a beer drinker or two."

This remark was met with even more laughter.

Jason shook his head. "The guy's got a few screws
loose."

"Afraid he might catch something?" Tisha gave him
a sly look.

"Yeah," Jason replied. "He might catch a cold coming out to check that trap in the middle of the winter.
And then we'll have some grumpy substitute teacher
who will give us even more homework than Tollifson
does." With a wave of one hand, Jason dismissed the
whole thing as silly. He looked around the crowd. "I

still don't see Holly," he said with a shake of his head. "But maybe . . ." He pulled away from Tisha and Zack and hurried to Mr. Tollifson's side.

By now the crowd was ready to forget Mr. Tollifson's experiment and get back to the celebration. Things were getting noisy again, and Jason had to yell to attract everyone's attention.

"Hey! Guys!" Jason raised his voice above the noise and waved his arms like a windmill. "Hey!" He tried again. "I'm looking for Holly Callison. You know, the new girl. The one with the red hair." Jason twirled around, giving the entire circle a quick look. "Holly? Are you here?"

There was no answer.

"Anyone seen Holly?" he asked no one in particular.

The answer came from a surprising place.

"Yeah, I saw her." Laila stepped into the circle. The bonfire was beginning to die down. The flames had settled from yellow to orange and Laila's face shone with the light of them, bronzed and gleaming. She seemed pleased by something, surprised. She even smiled.

"I saw Holly about fifteen minutes ago," she said, looking from Jason out to the edges of the Hollow. "She was sitting over there. A couple minutes later . . ." Laila lifted her shoulders, the gesture graceful and as careless as a cat's leisurely stretch. "A couple minutes later, she was gone."

"Thanks for nothing." Jason couldn't keep the disappointment out of his voice. "We know she's gone," he said. "What we're trying to find out is where she went." He spun away from Laila and headed back to where Tisha and Zack waited for him.

"If you weren't so impatient maybe you would find out."

Laila's statement slammed into Jason's back. She sounded as cranky as a kid who'd just had a favorite toy taken away.

Jason stopped in his tracks. He felt guilty for letting his worry about Holly eclipse his good manners. He'd pushed aside Laila's offer of help too quickly and now he owed her an apology.

He turned back to her, the words ready on his lips.

They died there as soon as he saw Laila's face.

She didn't look nearly as mad as she sounded. She was smiling, a small, odd half-smile that made her look like she'd just tasted something she liked very much.

Laila let the suspense mount. Her chin up, the color high in her cheeks, she let the moment drag on.

Finally she sighed as if she was bored with the game. "I saw where she went," Laila said. She tossed her head so that her glossy mane of black hair slithered over her shoulders like silk.

"Holly went into the woods."

The top stair gave way as soon as Holly stepped on it.

Her right hand instinctively grabbed for a handrail that wasn't there, and she flew down the next three steps and landed on her hands and knees.

She heard her jeans rip, felt the sting as the skin of

her knees and the palms of her hands scraped against rock and hard-packed ground.

She didn't stop to think about the pain or the hot, wet feel of the blood that oozed from her knees and trickled down the inside of her pant legs. She scrambled to her feet and took a few steps back, away from the camp building, her gaze fastened to the doorway.

It was empty. Just as empty now as it had been when she entered the building.

And yet . . .

Holly hauled in a deep breath to try and calm herself.

And yet she was sure she hadn't been alone in there.

Someone—Something—had been inside that building with her. Something that destroyed her reason and blocked her ability to think clearly. Something that triggered her deepest fears and sent her racing blindly into the night.

Something that was still watching her.

A chill twisted along Holly's shoulders.

Terrified she might see something there, but just as afraid not to look, she forced her eyes to the doorway again. From there, her gaze moved from window to window.

There was nothing.

The windows were as empty as the doorway.

Empty as the endless darkness of a nightmare, or the long, cold horror of a silent scream.

Holly tried to shake the thoughts from her mind. It didn't work.

A sour taste surged up from her stomach and into her mouth, the flavor of something unwanted and undesired. The taste of fear.

Holly took another step back.

It felt good to be away from the suffocating nearness of the ruined building.

The realization gave Holly a spark of hope and enough courage to force her legs to move. She retreated bit by bit, each movement reminding her that tomorrow she would have an assortment of blue-black bruises as painful souvenirs of her visit to the woods on Harper's Mountain.

Another few steps and she felt some of the heaviness lift from her chest and shoulders.

She drew in a breath. Let it out. Drew in another.

Then she turned and ran.

Holly raced through the woods as fast as she could, her gaze fastened to where the trees thinned and the light of the bonfire brightened the sky like the glow of a night-light that chased away the monsters hiding under a child's bed.

She was almost at the spot where the trees disappeared and the Hollow began when a pair of strong arms wrapped around her and hauled her to a stop.

Everything went black.

Holly felt her face get pressed into something warm and soft. She struggled for breath, straining to keep her head up, but the hold around her only tightened.

Holly beat her fists against the soft, warm thing and twisted in its arms. She clawed at it, and when she felt the smallest bit of bare flesh brush against her cheek, she seized the opportunity. She opened her mouth and bit down hard.

"Shoot! What the heck are you doing?"

Holly scrambled back and swept the hair out of her eyes.

Jason was standing not two feet away, his eyes as round as saucers. He was cradling his right wrist in his left hand.

"Jason! I'm sorry." All the desperate fear that had given Holly the courage to fight drained away. It was replaced with complete embarrassment. She took a step forward, her hands out to Jason in apology.

Jason took a step back. "You didn't have to bite me." He shook his wrist and squeezed his eyes shut. "Your teeth are as sharp as a cat's. What were you doing anyway, tearing through here like you were being chased by Godzilla? You didn't have a clue where you were going. You were headed right into that little creek." He pointed to a small, quick running stream that lay at the bottom of a two-foot embankment. "I was trying to keep you from falling."

"I know. I—" Holly looked from the creek to Jason and her eyes filled with tears. He looked angry, upset. And it was all her fault.

"I'm sorry," she said, the tears spilling into her voice. "I got lost and I thought . . . I thought . . ."

Holly couldn't finish the story. She was ashamed. She was relieved. And the mixture of the two emotions blocked her throat and left her tongue-tied.

There was nothing left to do but cry.

At the same time Holly told herself the decision was both childish and stupid, she knew she had to give in to it. Her tears rolled down her cheeks, hot and salty, and she let out a strangled sob that echoed in the vast stillness of the woods like the cry of a wounded animal.

In two quick steps, Jason closed the distance between them. His hands on her shoulders, he bent to look into her face.

All the anger dissolved from Jason's expression. His eyes darkened with concern. He wrapped one arm around Holly and gently drew her near. "What were you doing out here by yourself?"

Holly closed her eyes and rested her head against Jason's shoulder. The tears were coming faster now, making it hard to talk. "I heard Tisha calling me and I—"

"Tisha?" Jason smoothed one hand over her hair, his voice as tender as his touch. "Tisha was with me the whole time. We were looking for you. She and Zack are checking the area near the refreshment stands now."

Holly stiffened in Jason's arms. She looked up at him, sure she'd see some sign that he was joking.

But he wasn't. She could tell as much from the thin, hard line of Jason's mouth as from the way he looked down at her, his eyes clouded with confusion, as if he was a little afraid she was some kind of nutcase.

"She wasn't in the woods? Are you sure?"

Jason shook his head. "Tisha? In the woods? Think about it. Tisha's almost as afraid of the woods as I am of advanced trigonometry. You know she wouldn't come out here by herself."

"Yeah. I know." Holly nodded, turning the thought over in her mind.

"Was somebody else out there?"

Jason's question sounded hesitant, almost afraid, and Holly realized he must have been studying her mussed up hair and the holes in her jeans. "Did some-body—?"

She couldn't bear to see him worry. "No." Holly answered as quickly as she could. She couldn't help it. Jason's gentle concern made her smile. "There wasn't anyone."

Jason wrapped his free arm around Holly's waist and drew her closer. "Then what happened?"

Jason was soft and warm and she felt safe in his arms. Holly leaned her head against his shoulder and found the strength she needed in the steady, strong beating of his heart.

The terrors she had imagined in the woods were nothing more than that, she told herself, illusions brought on by her own fears and Tisha's scary stories. She hugged Jason back to thank him for his concern.

"Nothing happened," Holly said and, looking back on it, she realized she was telling the absolute truth. "Nothing at all. I went for a walk and I got lost. It won't happen again. I promise."

"Good." Jason let out a long sigh that brushed against her hair like the whisper of angel wings. He crooked one finger beneath her chin and raised her face to

his. "I was worried about you, Holly. I thought . . .
I mean, I know if something happened to you, I'd . . .
I mean . . ."

Even in the dark, Holly could tell that Jason was
blushing. The thought filled her with a warm rush of
affection. Raising herself on tiptoe, she planted a kiss
on Jason's cheek.

"Thanks," she said.

"Hope I'm not interrupting anything."

At the sound of the voice, Holly spun around.

His arms swinging at his sides, his stride loose and
easy, Alex Sarandon was coming through the woods
as if it was a fine spring day and he was off on a
leisurely walk. He stopped dead at the sight of Holly
and Jason and leaned back against the nearest tree. A
smile brightened his expression.

"Of course not!" Jason unwound his arms from
around Holly so quickly, he nearly tripped over his
own feet and went tumbling into the stream. At the
last moment he righted himself and had the decency
to look embarrassed.

Holly suspected it wasn't an act, and she was sure
he was trying to preserve her reputation, not his own.
Still, Jason's reaction made her feel like a naughty
child caught committing some minor violation of the
rules, and she didn't like the feeling at all.

She wondered if that was how Alex viewed her, like
an inexperienced child. The thought did little to soothe
emotions that had been on a roller coaster all night
long. It didn't help to realize Alex wasn't paying the
slightest bit of attention to anything Jason was doing
or saying.

His eyes were trained on Holly, directly on Holly, and if he noticed her messed up hair or her torn clothes or the bits and pieces of leaves and dirt that clung to her jacket like pieces of confetti, he didn't show it.

He turned his smile up a notch or two. "I can go away," he said with a meaningful look toward the Hollow. "And give you two some privacy."

"That's okay." Jason responded before Holly could. "We were just on our way back to the bonfire." And, with one hand on her back, he nudged Holly out of the woods.

6

It wasn't a sound that alerted Holly to the danger. It was a feeling. A Presence.

It pressed against her in the darkened library, more ominous than the thunderous silence, and sent a quiver through her that rattled her shoulders and caused her heart to begin a frantic thumping.

There was a book open on the table in front of her, and Holly closed it. She rose from her seat. Her chair scraped against the wooden floor and she winced, certain the sound was enough to betray her.

It would know where she was now.

The realization made Holly's blood run cold.

It would know where to find her.

"Take it easy, Callison." Holly's own voice sounded hollow in her ears, like it came from the bottom of a deep well. "Take it easy. If you're here at school, there must be others, too. Tisha's bound to be here. And Jason. If you can find them . . ."

It was an excellent plan and Holly congratulated herself. All she needed to do to put it into action was get out of the library.

She glanced around.

Although it was night, no one had bothered to turn

on any of the lights. The room was pitch-dark except for the faint light of the exit sign that glowed red above the doorway.

It wasn't a warm light, not like the cheery red bulbs on a Christmas tree. This light was an alarm signal. Red like the warning flashers of a fire engine. Red like blood.

A fluttering sensation began in Holly's stomach. She gulped it down and started toward the door.

That's when she saw it.

It was nothing more than a movement in the shadows near the door, like the shape she had seen in the ruined camp building, but it made her arms prickle with gooseflesh. This was the same Presence she'd sensed in the woods. She could feel it in her bones. Holly squinted into the darkness, trying to catch a glimpse of it.

Just like on Harper's Mountain, there was nothing to see. Nothing but a deeper darkness in the gloom, a shadow that was sleek and low to the ground. It twisted across the floor like black fog, curving and turning, dissolving and taking shape again, closing in on her.

Holly didn't wait to see more. The door to the third floor hallway was directly in front of her, and she squeezed her eyes shut and ran for it.

She didn't know how long it took to get to the door. She didn't feel herself hit it. But the next thing she knew, Holly was out in the corridor.

The library doors banged shut behind her and Holly leaned back against the cold metal. Whatever was in the library was locked tight inside. She smiled and let out a sigh. Whatever was inside could just stay there.

Still smiling, Holly headed for the stairway. Her feet were weightless. Her head felt giddy. She was dizzy with the joy of escaping whatever danger lurked inside the library, anxious to find Jason and get home.

"The newspaper office." She wasn't sure how she knew it, but Holly was certain that's where Jason would be. "I'll just go down to the first-floor newspaper office." Her voice echoed back at her in the corridor, but it didn't sound as scared now as it did relieved.

She was tempted to race down the stairs to find Jason, but why should she? There was nothing here to bother her now. Holly went down the first flight of stairs, humming the tune to a song she'd heard on the radio earlier in the day.

She turned the corner to head down the next flight of stairs and froze.

There was something at the bottom of the steps.

Holly's fingers tightened on the railing. She didn't see the shadow this time. She didn't see anything but two pinpoints of red, like the light of the exit signs reflected in an animal's eyes.

And she knew.

She knew the Presence was there, waiting for her.

She couldn't go down, and there was no use going back up. Holly turned and raced into the second-floor corridor.

There was a light on in the biology lab. It spilled from the window in the door, its soft yellow glow inviting Holly to safety. Certain the Presence would not dare to come into the light, she slowed her steps and reached for the doorknob.

The room was locked.

Holly peered into the window. Tisha was inside. So was Mr. Tollifson. They were examining an animal skeleton that was laid out on the table in the front of the room.

"Tisha!" Holly knocked on the door. "Tisha, it's me. Open the door."

Tisha looked up and waved. Mr. Tollifson peered over his glasses at Holly. But they didn't come to the door. They went right back to looking at the animal skeleton.

"Tisha!" Holly tapped on the window. "I'm not kidding, Tisha. I need to get in. There's something out here and—"

Holly's words were cut off by a snarl, a low rumble that reverberated through the halls like the boom of a cannon.

She pounded on the door.

Tisha didn't even look up.

Holly rested her head against the glass of the door. She closed her eyes, sure that when she opened them again, everything would be all right.

Tisha would open the door and show her in. The lights would be back on and everything in the school would look as harmless as ever. The Presence would be gone.

Slowly she lifted her head and opened her eyes.

The lights in the corridor were still off. So were the lights in the biology lab. Tisha wasn't there anymore. Nobody was.

Holly glanced down the corridor toward the stairway.

The shadow wasn't a shadow anymore. It had grown and solidified, and it sat there in the doorway, the light of the red exit sign gleaming around it like a halo of fire.

It was a panther. A huge black panther.

Holly sucked in a ragged breath. She tried to scream, but no sound came from her mouth. She tried to run, but her feet refused to follow the advice of her head. She stood rooted to the spot and stared.

The cat didn't move. It sat there, its magnificent head erect, its ears pricked, its slender tail swishing back and forth in time to the pulse of Holly's heart. Its eyes glowed at her through the darkness, small and red, hotter than any fire. Its long tongue flicked from between powerful jaws to reveal its canine teeth, long, and white and as sharp as knives.

There was something about the look of those teeth that goaded Holly into action. Without turning her back on the panther, she moved away, each step slow and careful.

The panther sat perfectly still, watching. Just watching.

Holly backed away a few more steps. There was a door on her right, the chemistry lab, and she tried the knob. The room was locked. The next classroom door was locked, too. And the next.

Finally, she came to the connecting hallway where the art and music rooms were located. She dodged into the corridor.

Now that she was away from the panther's fiery eyes, Holly seemed to regain her senses. She drew in a breath and, darting to the stairway at the end of the hall, she scrambled down the stairs.

Her luck held. She made it to the first floor.

The school newspaper office was near the main doors and Holly headed toward it instinctively. There was a light on inside.

"Jason!" Holly pounded on the door. "Jason, let me in."

The door snapped open and Holly dashed inside.

There was a high stool set in front of the nearest layout table. Certain her knees wouldn't hold her another second, Holly hurried to it and sat down. She dropped her head into her hands, fighting back the cold terror that turned her stomach. After a moment, her heartbeat slowed. She drew in a breath and scooped her hair out of her eyes.

"Jason, thanks. I—"

Holly looked up. Jason wasn't there. But Alex Sarandon was. Alex Sarandon who had never said more than two words to her. Alex Sarandon whose behavior had been so mysterious and so abrupt. Alex Sarandon who was everything she'd ever dreamed of in a boy and who always acted like she was invisible.

Alex Sarandon was smiling down at her, smiling as

if he knew she would be there, smiling as if he had been waiting for her.

"I didn't think you'd come." He took a step nearer, his green eyes glimmering with a light as warm as summer sunshine. "I didn't think you'd know I was here."

"I had to come." Holly was out of breath. Her voice shook. "Alex, there's something out in the corridor. Something that followed me." Holly looked toward the door. Alex had left it open. She bolted from her chair and took a step toward it, her hand out.

"Don't." Alex intercepted her before she got as far as the door. He took her hand and wound his fingers through hers. "You don't need to worry," he said, his voice as soft as his touch. "I'm here."

Alex looked like a million bucks. His hair shone like the finest drawing ink, liquid and black. His eyes glimmered from beneath lashes so thick and long, they'd surely be the envy of any self-respecting model.

He was dressed in jeans that fit him like a second skin. His shirt was open at the neck. Holly watched the small, round patch at the base of his throat where his heart beat against his skin.

"You look great." Alex held her at arm's-length and looked her up and down. His smile widened and he winked at her. "Good enough to eat."

Holly looked down at herself. For the first time, she realized she was wearing a nightgown. It was her favorite white cotton gown, the one with the pink rosebuds embroidered at the neck. It crossed her mind to wonder what on earth she was doing at school in her nightgown, but Holly didn't have time to think about it.

Alex pulled her into his arms and every other thought flew out of her head.

His purple dress shirt was crisp beneath her fingers. His hands were gentle where they pressed against the small of her back. He was warm and comforting and Holly felt safe in the circle of his arms.

Alex crooked one finger beneath her chin and raised her face so that her mouth was only inches from his. "You don't have to be afraid," he said. "Not anymore."

Holly wanted to believe him. She wanted to believe the eager look of longing in his eyes, the provocative smile that played around his lips, the tenderness of the soft breath he brushed against her lips.

She closed her eyes and tilted her head back.

As suddenly as she did, Alex was gone.

Holly opened her eyes. She was alone.

The door of the newspaper office was still open and she looked out into the hallway. The school was lit like a birthday cake. Lights blazed from the overhead fixtures. The security lights were on. Every classroom door was open, every light was lit.

But there was no one around.

Holly looked across the corridor to the wall where the panther mural was painted.

LOS GATOS PANTHERS. The words were still there in large, bright letters. But the panther was gone.

The wall was empty.

The Presence was still loose in the building.

"Wake up! You're dreaming. Holly! Holly!"

Holly bolted up in bed.

Her white cotton nightgown was soaked with sweat. Her heart was beating double time. Tisha was kneeling on the floor next to her bed, shaking her with all her might.

"Hey! It was just a dream." To be sure she was getting through to her, Tisha shook her one more time. "Are you okay? Holly? Are you awake?"

"Huh?" Holly blinked, fighting her way back from a sleep so deep, she would have sworn the things that had happened in it were more real than a dream. The dark memories of the nightmare still floated through her consciousness. Holly kneaded her fingers over her face and rubbed her eyes to try to make the images disappear.

Even this little bit of a response seemed to be enough to relieve some of Tisha's worries. She sat back on her heels. "You were twisting and kicking so much, you woke me up." She yawned and stretched. "That must have been some dream."

"Yeah." Holly admitted that much, but she wasn't sure how much more she wanted to say.

"And?" Tisha raised herself on her knees and gave Holly the kind of look she always used when she was after information. She looked just like a small, feisty dog on the trail of a hot scent.

"And you think I should tell you every little thing

just because you camped out on my bedroom floor last night?" Holly tried to keep her voice cheery, her comment light. She peered down to where Tisha sat on her army-green sleeping bag and grinned, hoping that meant an end to the subject.

Tisha didn't buy it. Her lips thinned, and one corner of her mouth pulled into an expression that was almost a cynical smirk.

"No, I don't think you should tell me every little thing because I camped out on your bedroom floor last night." Tisha's voice was as sour as her look. "I think you should tell me because something happened at the bonfire two nights ago, something that's been bothering you ever since. I think you should tell me because I'm your best friend and best friends share their secrets and their troubles. And because if you don't tell me, you're going to be just as miserable at the dance tonight as you were at the football game last night. Don't deny it! You were way too quiet."

"I had a great time last night." Even to her own ears, Holly's defense sounded a little too forced. She had no choice, she told herself. She wasn't ready to admit that she couldn't forget the strange incident on Harper's Mountain two nights ago. But she couldn't tell anyone about it, either. Not even Tisha.

It was still all too real. All too frightening. All too impossible to explain. She couldn't forget it, not even in her sleep. Why else would she have had the disturbing dream?

She needed time. Time to sort it all out. And the only way to gain that time was to steer Tisha clear of all talk of Harper's Mountain.

"I didn't see Jason complaining about the way I acted last night." Holly dangled the change of subject in front of Tisha like a fisherman offering a juicy worm.

She bit at it. "Jason wouldn't notice if you sprouted two heads and wings and started talking Chinese," Tisha said. "He's so crazy about you, he's just happy to be with you."

The words hurt. Not because they weren't true, but because they were, and Holly knew it.

Avoiding the critical look Tisha was giving her, Holly picked at one corner of her blanket.

"I promised myself I'd have fun at the football game last night," Holly said, her voice small and apologetic. "I tried. I'm sorry if it didn't work. I swear I won't let the same thing happen at the dance tonight. I don't want to spoil your fun. Or Jason's."

Even this much of an apology wasn't enough to suit Tisha. She leaned nearer. "Oh? You're thinking about Jason? That's a real switch."

"That's not fair." Holly grabbed her pillow and hurled it across the room. She was mad at Tisha for confronting her. Mad at herself for not being able to control her emotions, and her affections, and her irritating fixation with Alex. "I like Jason," she said. "You know I do."

When Tisha saw how miserable Holly looked, some of the disapproval faded from her expression. "I know you like Jason," she said. "But not the way he wants you to like him."

With one fist, Holly pounded the bed. "It's not

my fault, Tisha. I've tried. I really have. I do like Jason. As a friend. I wish I could like him more. If only . . ."

"If only you could stop thinking about Alex Sarandon?"

All the disappointment and confusion of the last few weeks peaked in Holly and she let out a shriek of frustration. "It's not like me," she said, trying to explain to Tisha what she couldn't even explain to herself. "I'm usually so . . . so . . . ." She searched for the right word. " . . . So sensible," she finally said. "I'm sensible and clearheaded. But when Alex is around . . ."

Holly felt a swift wave of heat color her cheeks. "See?" She pointed to her face. "I can't even think about him without turning into a puddle of mush. How can he ever get to like me if he never sees the real me? It's driving me nuts."

Holly sighed and flopped back against the mattress. "That dream I had . . . ? It was . . . It was . . . I had a dream that Alex kissed me. Well, almost kissed me."

"What!" The word escaped Tisha with a whoosh. She looked as stunned as if someone had just pulled the rug out from under her or, in this case, the sleeping bag. Plopping onto the floor, she shook her head back and forth until it bobbed like one of those statues with springs where their necks should be.

"You've got it bad," Tisha said. "Real bad. Holly, I told you before, steer clear of him. I know you'll be sorry if you don't."

"It's not like I haven't tried!" Holly jumped out of bed and paced her room. She went all the way to the windows and back again before she spoke. "I know what you're going to say. Alex likes girls who are pretty. And I'm not. I'm a freckle-faced, redhead who will never be sleek and gorgeous like Amber, or Lindsey, or Laila."

Tisha was trying to say something, but Holly wouldn't let her. She held up one hand for silence and continued. "And I know what else you're going to say. Alex likes girls who are sophisticated. And I'm not. I still feel like I could die every time I think about him seeing me and Jason in the woods together." By this time, Holly had gathered so much steam, she wasn't about to stop.

"I know. I know." She paced from her dresser, to her bed, to the windows and back again. "Alex likes girls who can look him in the eyes without having their knees turn to rubber, girls who can actually carry on a conversation with him. Not ones like me, ones who feel dumb as a post every time he walks by. I know what you're going to say, Tisha. I am very definitely not Alex Sarandon's type."

Holly stopped her pacing long enough to haul in a long breath.

"Then why can't I stop thinking about him?" She threw her hands in the air, asking the question of Tisha as well as of herself. "I feel guilty every time I'm with Jason. I feel miserable every time I see Alex. Tisha, what's wrong with me?"

Tisha didn't answer. She came over to where Holly was standing and put one hand on her shoulder. "What you need," she said, "is a dose of Grammy's medicine.

The same one she gave to me when I was eating too much chocolate a few summers ago."

The comment was so completely off the subject, Holly had to laugh. She turned to Tisha, a question on her face. "Chocolate?" Holly asked.

"Yep." Tisha padded over to the bed and sat down on the edge. Her legs dangled and she kicked her feet up and down. "The summer I was thirteen," she said, "I started to eat every bit of chocolate in sight. I don't know why. It just tasted good. It was all I could think about. Chocolate. I had to have chocolate. Grammy's not the type who usually cares about things like that. She isn't strict or anything. She's never refused me anything in the whole time I've lived with her and that's been since my folks died when I was little." Tisha gave her a funny sort of embarrassed smile.

"But you know all that. Anyway" —she settled herself, prepared to tell the rest of the story— "Grammy knew it wasn't good for me. So she cured me the way we're going to cure you of this obsession with Alex."

"We are?" It was all so absurd, Holly couldn't help but be curious. She sat down next to Tisha. "And what are we going to do?"

"What Grammy did," Tisha explained. "She left chocolate all over the house. Candy bars, cupcakes, cookies . . . you name it. I'd find it in the living room, or on the kitchen table, or in the cupboards. For a week or so, I was in chocolate heaven!" Tisha grinned at the memory.

"What did you do?" Holly asked.

Tisha's grin turned into a smile. "What else could I do? I ate it. All of it. Until about the fourth or fifth day. After that, I was so full of chocolate I couldn't stand the sight of it. I still eat it. Occasionally. But it isn't the obsession it used to be. So you see, that's what we'll do with Alex."

Holly ran her hands through her hair. "I must still be asleep," she said. "What are we going to do with Alex? Leave him in the living room and on the kitchen table and in the cupboards until I can't stand looking at him anymore?"

"No." Tisha got up and went over to the closet. Holly's new dress was hanging on the door, ready for tonight's homecoming dance.

The dress was dark green satin with a flared skirt that came just to the top of Holly's knees. It was strapless, but not low-cut enough to horrify either Holly's mom or dad. It was topped with a short-cropped jacket studded with rhinestone buttons.

Tisha ran her fingers over the silky skirt. "You're going to look gorgeous tonight." Her expression brightened and her eyes sparkled with the excitement of her plan. "We'll do your hair up real special. What were you going to do, wear it down?" She didn't wait for Holly to answer. "We'll braid it. Yeah. With maybe some kind of sparkly stuff in your hair. And then when you go to the dance, you'll act like Laila usually acts, you know, the center of attention. You'll laugh the loudest and dance the fastest and look the best. You'll act like the queen of the place. Alex is bound to notice you then."

Holly still wasn't sure where all this was going. "And once he does?" she asked.

"Once he notices you, he's bound to fall head over heels for you. And once he does that" —Tisha brushed her hands together— "I guarantee you won't want him anymore. It's just like the chocolate, don't you see? Once you can have all you want, you don't want it anymore." Her mind made up, Tisha rolled her sleeping bag into a tight bundle and set it against the wall.

"This is going to be fun," she said. "We're going to have a great time and Alex Sarandon . . ." Tisha's face lit with a mischievous smile. "Alex Sarandon is bound to notice you."

7

"It's not working."

Holly dropped into the chair next to Tisha's. Her feet hurt. She was thirsty. She was tired of dancing every dance and laughing at every joke and playing a role she was not happy or comfortable with.

She looked across the gym to where Alex sat with his arm around Amber's shoulders. He looked distracted. His gaze roamed around the gym like that of the animals Holly had seen in the zoo. Restless. Bored. He looked as subdued as the dark suit he was wearing, as sedate as the tasteful pattern of his red-and-gray-striped tie. Like he was waiting for something exciting to happen. Like he was sure it would never happen here.

Holly sighed. "He hasn't given me a second glance."

"I noticed." Tisha sighed. "I don't get it. It can't be you. You look terrific. You really do. If you need proof, keep an eye on Laila. Every time she looks over here, she sneers. She's jealous, the little witch. And it sure isn't of me."

"Oh, I don't know." Holly studied the way Tisha's red-sequined dress shimmered in the light. "You look pretty good yourself."

Tisha wasn't listening. Hard at work thinking, she propped her elbows on the table and cradled her chin in her hands. "Maybe something's wrong with Alex," she suggested. "Maybe he needs his eyes checked or something."

Holly laughed. "Yeah. Maybe he doesn't recognize the queen of the dance when he sees her." Her words were more nonchalant than the way she felt. She felt aggravated. Aggravated at Tisha for talking her into this ridiculous scheme. Aggravated at Alex for not falling for it. Aggravated at herself for letting the whole thing bother her.

"I got you something to drink."

Jason came up to the table carrying two large Cokes and Holly's mood brightened. She may not have attracted Alex's attention this evening, but it was obvious she was making quite an impression on Jason. He lit up like a Christmas tree every time he looked at her.

Jason handed one Coke to Holly and sipped the other. "I'm glad you're having a good time," he said.

It was true, Holly realized. She was having a good time. In spite of Tisha's corny plan and Alex's indifference, she was having fun.

The music was great. The dancing was wonderful. Even the dinner provided by the cafeteria had been pretty good. Some of the gloom that had surrounded Holly since that night at the bonfire seemed to lift and she smiled.

She took a drink of her Coke and studied the way the lights made Jason's blond hair shine like the sun.

In spite of all the cruel things Laila had said, Jason looked handsome in his navy blue sportcoat. He was wearing it with a pair of gray pants and a blue shirt. He might have looked like a lawyer or a preppy college student if it wasn't for his tie. Unlike Alex's very proper tie, Jason's was wide and wild. Holly squinted at it, trying to bring the pattern into focus. It wasn't really a plaid. It wasn't really a stripe. It looked more like an abstract painting, one that contained every color in the rainbow. It suited Jason's personality perfectly.

"Aha! What's this I hear? A song we have to dance to."

Sometime while Holly was busy looking at Jason, the disc jockey had put on a slow song. Jason already had his hand on her arm and was tugging her to her feet and toward the dance floor when Mr. Tollifson came up to them.

He cupped his hand to his mouth and said something in Jason's ear.

Holly watched the excited smile vanish from Jason's face. He nodded and Mr. Tollifson disappeared back into the crowd.

Jason turned Holly's hand over in his. "I'm sorry," he said, a mix of emotions playing its way across his face.

He was embarrassed. Holly could tell from the way he refused to meet her eyes.

He was angry. She could tell that from the way he pressed his lips together.

He was disappointed. He threw a look from the

crowd of students dancing slow and close out on the
floor to Holly in her shimmering green dress.

"It's my dad." Jason let out a long sigh of frustration
that said, without a doubt, this was not the first time
this sort of thing had happened. "He passed out on
the kitchen floor. I know I should just leave him
there, teach him a lesson. But my mom never would.
She'll try to move him by herself, just so my little
sister doesn't see him there in the morning. Mom just
called and . . ."

"It's okay," Holly squeezed Jason's hand and offered
as much of a smile as she could manage. "I understand.
You want me to wait here for you?"

Holly's offer relieved Jason of the choice between
her and his family. Like the sun coming out from
behind a cloud, his face brightened. "Would you?"
he asked. "Would you mind? I mean, I could be back
in a half hour or so, as soon as we get Dad up and
into bed. I'd hate to have to take you home so early
and . . . I'd hate to spoil your evening and . . . I was
hoping we'd go out for a burger after or a whatever
you vegetarians eat and—"

"I'll be right here waiting for you," Holly promised.
She was smiling in earnest now. She looked over to
where Tisha and Zack were dancing. "I've got plenty
of company. And if all else fails, I can always go talk
to Mr. Tollifson."

"Yeah, that would be great." Jason grinned. "I'll
bet the other chaperons won't even talk to him." He
shifted from foot to foot, prolonging the good-byes.
"Okay then, I'll get going."

"Go." With a gentle shove, Holly urged him toward the door. "The sooner you leave, the sooner you'll get back."

Still smiling, she watched Jason make his way through the crowd and out the door. It was a shame a nice guy like Jason had to handle a problem as difficult as a father who was a drinker.

The edges of Holly's smile melted at the thought.

It was a shame—

"Would you like to dance?"

The sound of a voice close to her ear caught Holly completely off guard. She spun around and found her nose up against the middle of a guy's tie.

A proper, businesslike tie.

One with red and gray stripes.

Holly swallowed hard.

She forced her eyes up from the tie. Up past a crisp white shirt. Up to a square jaw, and past a finely shaped chin and over a well-proportioned nose. Up to eyes as green as grass in June.

She couldn't have looked any farther if she wanted to.

Holly's gaze held and stuck, just like her voice was sticking in her throat, and her blood was buzzing in her brain, and the sight of Alex's face was spinning in front of her eyes.

"Maybe you didn't hear me, I asked if you'd like to dance."

Alex didn't wait for her to answer. One hand on her elbow, he ushered her out onto the dance floor.

The same song was still playing. The music was

slow, the rhythm spellbinding. Alex took Holly's right hand in his left and settled his own right hand on the smooth curve where her waist met her hips.

He looked down at her. "I'm Alex Sarandon," he said.

"Yes, I know." Holly had to force herself not to cringe openly. What an incredibly stupid thing to say! She might as well have confessed that she'd been spying on him since the first day of school.

"I mean, I know who you are because you're in a couple of my classes. I think." She bit her lower lip and hoped she didn't sound as witless to Alex as she did to herself. She hurried on before he could notice. "Biology, right? Second period with Mr. Tollifson. And American history. And because of the game last night, of course. I know who you are because of the game. You were really good. I don't think we would've won if you didn't pick up that fumble and run the ball in for a touchdown."

Alex shrugged off the compliment. "And you're Holly Callison. Newly arrived from Cleveland. Budding artist. I've seen your drawings hanging up in the art corridor. Friend of Tisha who knows all and tells all. Pizza lover. Too shy to talk to me even though I've tried a few times. You're here with Jason Van Kirk, aren't you?"

The mention of Jason's name made Holly feel like a traitor. Even though she knew it was far too soon for Jason to be back, she glanced over her shoulder.

Alex seemed amused by her anxious look. A slow smile inched up the corners of his mouth. "Jason's a nice boy," he said.

He didn't have to finish the rest of the statement. Holly knew exactly what he was implying. Jason was a nice boy. But Alex? Alex was a man.

The thought did little to calm the excitement that fluttered its way around Holly's stomach and made her feel like she was about to go spinning up to the ceiling, like a balloon sent flying by the prick of a pin. She drew in a tight breath and caught the scent of Alex's aftershave. It smelled like a forest at night, mossy and mysterious, shadowy, subtle, and so masculine, it took her breath away.

The smell seemed to overpower her reasoning at the same time it heightened her senses.

The sound of the music sharpened in Holly's ears; the rhythm coursed through her blood. Alex's fingers wound through hers, and she felt his heartbeat telegraphed through his fingertips, each pulse in perfect measure to her own.

Did he feel the same things?

Holly dared to raise her eyes to Alex's face. He didn't look nearly as bored now as he had when he sat with his arm around Amber. He smiled down at her and a faint flicker of light stirred somewhere deep within his eyes until they gleamed like polished emeralds.

The song was nearly over and suddenly Holly realized she couldn't wait. She was getting more lightheaded by the second. She felt like a drowning person going down for the third time. Her pulse beat painfully in her temples. Her lungs ached. Her heart was pounding so loud, she was sure Alex could hear it.

She wouldn't have been able to take a deep breath even if she dared. It seemed as if all the oxygen had been sucked out of the gym. It had taken with it all the kids, all the chaperons, all the volunteer workers.

Only Holly and Alex remained, alone in a sphere of their own making where nothing could enter, nothing escape.

The music stopped, or maybe it stopped a long time ago and Holly never noticed.

Anxious to free herself from the strange, mesmerizing spell of Alex's eyes, she jerked to a standstill and pulled away.

"They're bound to play a fast song now." Holly's excuses were racing as fast as her heart. "The DJ has been doing that all evening. One slow song, a bunch of fast ones. I'm not much of a fast dancer and I—"

"Oh, I don't know." Alex didn't let go of Holly's hand. He tightened his hold over her fingers. As if he was thinking very hard, he narrowed his eyes and looked over to where the DJ sat thumbing through his selection of recordings. "Somehow I don't think that's going to hold true. Not this time."

He was right. The music started. It was another slow song.

"What good luck." Alex slid his hand back to Holly's waist. "Looks like we'll be able to stay out here a little while longer."

Holly couldn't have objected if she wanted to.

Alex flattened his hand against her back and none of the things she was worried about seemed to matter anymore. Not the sensation that she couldn't breathe, or the idea that she couldn't think straight, or the realization that if Jason came back and saw them dancing this close together, his feelings were sure to be hurt.

None of it mattered.

Swaying to the music, Holly relaxed in Alex's arms. He obviously took that as a good sign. He pulled her closer.

Holly glanced down to where Alex's hand lay against the silky fabric of her skirt. "Won't Amber mind?"

"Amber." Alex's lips curved into an expression that wasn't quite a smile. "We're not really here together. I mean, we're here. Together. But we're not really . . ." His explanation got feebler by the second. Alex knew it. His face split into the kind of embarrassed grin that made Jason look so adorable. On Alex, the expression wasn't the least bit adorable. It was devastating, and it made Holly's knees feel weak.

"Amber will find something to amuse herself with," Alex said, leaning nearer. "She's probably over in some corner gossiping with my little sister."

"Little?" The word struck Holly as odd. She shifted her head so that Alex was forced to look down at her. "I thought you guys were twins."

"We are. But I'm two-and-a-half minutes older. And that makes me the big brother. Sometimes Laila forgets."

Alex tugged Holly back against him. Obviously, he was ready to drop the subject.

But Holly wasn't. "Laila doesn't like me very much." She offered the comment to see what Alex would say.

Alex chuckled. "Of course she doesn't," he said. "She's jealous."

"Jealous!" Holly couldn't believe it. "You're kidding, right? Laila is the prettiest girl I've ever seen. She's the prettiest girl most people have ever seen. That's why she's got guys hanging around her constantly. I've never had that problem."

Alex stood up straight. He moved Holly far enough away so that he could look at her, from the elegant French braid in her hair to the sprinkle of freckles across her nose and cheeks. From there, he let his gaze flicker down to the rhinestone buttons on her jacket and the flared skirt of her dress.

His expression softened. His eyes lit with pleasure. "You're serious, aren't you? You really have no idea."

Holly was baffled. "No idea about what?"

"No idea how pretty you are." The way Alex said the words, they sounded less like flattery than they did a simple statement of fact. "You look great."

His comment sounded so much like the one he'd made to her in her dream, that Holly couldn't help but laugh. "Good enough to eat?" she asked.

As if someone had flicked a switch, all the dreaminess disappeared from Alex's face. He jerked to a stop so fast, Holly nearly fell over his feet. He recovered quickly and, both hands around her waist, he caught her just in time.

They steadied themselves, and fell back into the rhythm of the dance.

Alex didn't move his hands and after a second, Holly realized he wasn't going to. They rested against her waist, one hand on either hip, his thumbs brushing against the glossy fabric of her dress, his touch leaving a trail of fire that shot up to her throat and down to her stomach.

There wasn't much Holly could do with her own hands. Self-conscious, she glanced around. The other dancers sure didn't seem to be having the same problem. The guys had their hands tight around the girls' waists. The girls had their arms linked around the guys' necks.

Holly had no choice. She slid her hands up Alex's chest and wrapped them around his neck, her fingers linked together through the velvety strands of his hair that fell over the back of his collar.

"Good enough to eat?" Alex rolled the words over his tongue, his mouth close to Holly's ear. "It's kind of a strange thing to say. What would make you think of a thing like that?"

Holly felt like a fool for even mentioning it, but there was no way out now. "Just something I dreamed," she said.

"Dreamed." Alex seemed to find this just as interesting. He moved back far enough to look into Holly's face. "You must have some very interesting dreams."

"Not really." Holly tried to slam the door shut on this topic before it could get opened further. "I come up to the school track a couple nights a week and do a few laps. By the time I get home, I'm usually so exhausted, I just fall into bed and don't dream anything at all."

Alex nodded. "Do you like to run?"

Finally, they were on safe ground.

Holly let go a breath of relief and smiled. "Have you ever felt like you were flying? That's what running is to me." She tipped her head back and closed her eyes. She could almost feel the air stream past her face the way it did when she was on the track, almost sense the quickening of her heartbeat, the flow of her blood. "When I'm running," she said, "I feel like I'm soaring through the sky, like I'm surfing the wind. I love to run. I feel like it's something I was born to do." She opened her eyes to find Alex staring at her. In her excitement, she'd almost forgotten he was there. Holly blushed and laughed self-consciously.

Alex returned her smile. "I like to run, too." From the way he said the words, she knew he understood her enthusiasm because he shared it. "And I like to watch other people run. I've seen you on the track during your gym period."

He didn't need to say anymore. His words made it clear that he'd been watching Holly since the first day of school just like she'd been watching him.

The realization sent a warm tickle of excitement through Holly that completely dissolved her shyness. For the first time, she did not shrink from Alex's green gaze. She met it. Straight on.

"I was a pretty fair athlete back in Cleveland," Holly said, and it was the truth. "I made the state finals last year in track and cross-country. I was a cheerleader, too. I'd like to try out for the LGH cheer-leaders but your sister's got a lock on who gets in and who doesn't. Let's face it, that leaves me out. I am planning on trying out for track in the spring."

"It would be a lot of fun." Alex nodded his approval. "And it's not like I don't think it's a good idea, but . . ."

"But?" There was something about the tone of his voice Holly didn't like. She waited for more.

Alex smiled a funny sort of apologetic half-smile, the expression transforming his face. "It's a pity you're so slow."

"Slow?" Holly's back stiffened. "What do you mean, slow? I—"

The words stuck in her throat when she realized Alex wasn't taking her seriously at all. He was laughing.

"You think it's funny?" Holly's anger soared. "I don't. I—"

"No, no. Wait a minute." Trying to soothe her rising temper, Alex rested one hand on her shoulder. "I'm not laughing at you. It's just that you're so . . . so . . ." He looked up to the spinning mirrored ball at the center of the dance floor, as if he would find the right word there. "So fiery," he finally said, looking back at Holly and smiling. "Maybe that's why you're a redhead. You go up in flames. I like that in a girl."

He was humoring her now and that was almost as bad as insulting her running ability.

Holly stopped dancing even before the music

stopped. When it did, the other kids on the dance floor started making their way toward the tables set up along the walls. Holly didn't pay the least bit of attention to them. Not even when Tisha walked by and stared at her with her mouth open.

"Okay," Holly said, moving out of Alex's arms and glaring up at him. "I'll tell you what. I'll race you."

"What!" Alex's surprise was genuine.

"I'll race you," Holly said again. "Anytime. Anywhere. You name it."

Alex's smile disappeared and a flash of green fire flickered in his eyes in response to the challenge. "A race." He repeated the words as if he could taste them. "All right." He stuck out his right hand. "Tomorrow night. Here at the school track. Eight o'clock?"

"Eight o'clock." Holly pumped his hand. She was so angry, she didn't even shiver at his touch, not even when he held onto her a little longer than he needed to.

"We'll see who's slow," she said.

Alex tipped his head back and laughed. "Oh, yes," he said. "We sure will." He was still laughing as he walked toward the other side of the gym.

He was halfway over there when Laila stormed up to him with Amber in tow. Laila said something Holly couldn't quite hear but it seemed pretty certain it wasn't something nice. Her mouth was pulled so tight, it looked like a slash of red against her pale skin. Her eyes sparked. With one hand, Laila gestured toward Amber who looked positively miserable. Amber's face was red and blotchy, her eyes were swollen like she'd been crying.

Alex waved both the girls away with a quick, impatient gesture. He pushed his hands into his pockets and continued on toward the door that led to the parking lot.

He didn't look back at Laila and Amber at all. Not even once.

But Holly could have sworn, right before he got to the door, he looked back at her. And when he did, he was still laughing.

— 8 —

The night wind howled through the deserted football stadium, snatching at Holly's jacket and whipping wayward strands of her ponytail against her cheek.

Turning her back, she braced herself against the stiff breeze. She glanced around, up toward the stands where row after row of empty bleachers rose into the night, their outlines spare and gaunt, like skeleton bones.

Alex felt a quiver around his mouth, a stirring that was almost a smile.

She didn't see him.

She couldn't. Not if he didn't want to be seen. He blended too well with the shadows and moved as silently as a whisper on the wind.

He sat back and watched Holly slip out of her jacket and drape it over the nearest railing. The thin light of a quarter moon was more than enough for him to see that she was wearing purple shorts and a short-sleeved T-shirt the color of ripe raspberries.

Alex let his gaze wander from Holly's bare arms to her bare legs, from her coppery hair to her white sneakers. Even in workout gear, she looked as pretty tonight as she had last night in her shimmering green dress.

"Good enough to eat."

The memory of Holly's peculiar comment made Alex's canine teeth tingle. He flicked his tongue across his mouth to control the sensation.

Holly looked good enough to eat, all right, but that wasn't what he had in mind.

Not for Holly Callison.

There were more interesting things in this world, more interesting even than drinking human blood, though most were not nearly as satisfying.

Interesting.

That's what he had in mind for Holly.

Alex chuckled, the vibration rumbling through his chest and into his throat, almost a purr.

He slid from his place in the shadows, and slipped down the steps, closer to the running track.

If Holly was impatient or nervous waiting for him, she didn't show it. She went through a series of precise stretching exercises, completely unaware that he was watching her every move.

Another few steps closer. Alex paused. His nostrils flared.

Holly may have looked calm, but the aroma of her excitement was unmistakable.

The awareness sizzled up Alex's spine and along his back. He sucked in a long, deep breath and the scent stuck fast at the back of his throat. It was so distinct, he could taste it, so thrilling, it crackled through his blood and made every hair on the back of his neck stand on end.

Holly was nervous. She was excited.

Excited about meeting him.

The realization was too much even for Alex to control. Before he could stop himself, he was closing the distance between them, his strides long and graceful, his footfalls completely silent.

Down the bleacher steps, onto the track.

He ran, smooth and even, his passing barely noticeable except for the shadows that undulated like the waves of shifting heat around a fire.

He ran, one with nature and the wind and the night, and pulled himself to a stop not three feet behind Holly.

Was it instinct or hunger that urged him to pounce? Was it something else, some other appetite he did not fully understand?

Alex didn't know. He knew only that his body prickled with the messages being sent from his brain. His heart pounded. His mouth tingled. His muscles tensed, poised and ready.

He fought the blind impulse. With more willpower than he knew he possessed, Alex controlled the desire to leap and the need to grab hold and the longing to feed.

Controlled it.

And changed effortlessly into the shape Holly expected to see.

"What? No audience?"

At the sound of Alex's voice, Holly gasped and spun around.

Though she hadn't heard him come up, Alex was right behind her.

"Sorry." He smiled, his teeth gleaming white in the light of a sliver of a moon. "I didn't mean to startle you. I was just looking around as I came into the stadium." He cast a glance at the empty bleachers. "No Tisha? No Jason? I can't believe you didn't bring along your fans."

"I see you didn't either."

Holly recovered as quickly as she could and congratulated herself for sounding far more composed than she felt. She glanced over Alex's shoulder. "I thought you and Laila were joined at the hip."

There was no missing the sarcasm in Holly's voice. Alex's smile got wider.

"Laila's doing her hair." He brushed aside the subject with a lift of his shoulders. He laughed. "Or is it her nails?"

"Jason's working. He doesn't know I'm here." Holly knew she didn't owe Alex an explanation. Still, she couldn't seem to stop herself. "He stocks the shelves over at Mueller's Drug Store in the evening, you know. He wants to be a pharmacist and . . ."

She'd said too much already. Holly's words faded and she felt her face get hot.

Alex didn't seem to notice.

"And Tisha?" he asked.

"Tisha doesn't know I'm here, either. She wouldn't approve."

"Really?" Just when Holly thought Alex's smile couldn't get any more stunning, he turned it up. "Of track and field events? Or of me?"

It was impossible to lie when he was looking at her

this way. "I don't think Tisha has any complaints about running," Holly said. "My being here with you . . . that's another story."

"She doesn't like me." Alex didn't seem the least bit concerned with Tisha's opinion of him. He slipped out of his jacket and hung it on the railing next to Holly's. He extended one leg, bent his knee and stretched his calf muscles. "I have a sneaking feeling she's been listening to too much of her own gossip," he said. "I can just imagine the kinds of things she's told you about me." Alex stretched the other leg.

The comment didn't seem to deserve an answer, so Holly didn't give one. She jogged over to where the starting line was marked with white paint on the track.

Alex took the lane next to hers.

"Once around?" he asked.

Holly looked out to where the curve of the oval track disappeared into the inky shadows. "Once around," she agreed. "Right back here. I'll be waiting for you when you get here."

"Don't be so sure." Alex bent one knee to the ground in a sprinter's stance. "Ready?" he asked. "On my count of three. One. Two. Three!"

The last word was barely out of Alex's mouth when Holly dashed off the starting line.

It was a good start.

She congratulated herself.

It was a strong start.

Conserving energy, Holly paced herself, saving what

she could for the last length of track when she would put on one final burst of speed.

When they came to the first curve, she was still ahead of Alex. She could hear him a couple paces behind her, his breathing deep and even like her own, his steps light and steady on the dirt track.

"That was a nice little warm-up." How Alex caught up so quickly, Holly couldn't imagine. Suddenly, he was right there beside her, smiling over his shoulder at her. "Are you ready to really run now?"

He didn't wait for her to answer.

In a flash of speed, Alex pulled ahead.

Far ahead.

Holly slowed down, amazement destroying her concentration, anger blocking her throat and strangling every breath.

Alex had been teasing her. She knew that now. He let her get a head start to give her a false sense of confidence.

Holly peered into the darkness. Up ahead, she could just see Alex, his lean, athletic body moving effortlessly as if running was as natural to him as breathing or eating. He ran with his back straight, his head high, drinking in the rushing air and the black night in slow, steady breaths, his arms pumping methodically at his sides, his legs rising and falling to the rhythm of the race.

For a moment, Holly couldn't do anything but watch. Alex's movements were superb, liquid. He surprised her with his grace, amazed her with his speed. In less than a heartbeat, he was so far ahead, Holly knew she would never be able to catch up.

There was only one thing to do, Holly told herself. She should quit. Right here. Right now.

It was the only logical thing to do. The only smart thing to do. The only way she could save face.

With a snort and a stinging comment to herself, Holly ignored her own advice.

She ran harder, ran until her blood drove through her body and hammered in her heart. She ran until her ears pounded and her lungs ached and the scrapes on her knees that she'd gotten the night of the bonfire started bleeding all over again. She kept on running, even after she saw Alex cross the finish line.

She crossed the line herself, a full ten strides after he did. Her hands on her knees, she bent over and tried her best to catch her breath.

That was nearly impossible.

Holly drew in a huge breath of air, and another, and another. Nothing could slow the frantic beating of her heart or ease the tightness in her chest.

It didn't help when Alex sauntered up and smiled down at her, some curious emotion sparkling from his eyes. It might have been admiration, or maybe it was just astonishment, or amusement.

Maybe he was just shocked that she could be so stupid.

Holly tossed the thought aside. She forced herself to stand up straight and meet Alex's look head-on.

He wasn't even breathing hard.

Holly cursed him under her breath.

He didn't look tired. Not one hair on his head was

out of place. He looked relaxed, even a little bored, like he'd just come in from a leisurely walk where he didn't see anything of any interest at all.

Alex didn't say a thing. He tipped his head, studying Holly with an openness so obvious, it caused her already erratic heartbeat to skip a few counts.

He moved a step closer and, crooking one finger beneath her chin, tipped Holly's face up to his.

"Oh, Holly!" His voice as mysterious as the night, Alex breathed the words against her lips.

His touch left her helpless. It spiraled through her and curled around her heart and warmed places Holly never even knew existed. She reacted like a tender flower bud responds to the sun, leaning toward him, vulnerable and obedient.

Alex straightened, smiled, tapped her chin.

"It looks like you're going to have to run a lot faster to catch me," he said.

And with that, he turned, grabbed his jacket, and was out of the stadium before Holly could recover.

The dream was even worse than last time.

Holly scrambled from her bed, her head still dizzy with the memories of the nightmare.

She stared down at her sweat-soaked pillow and the blankets, twisted and kicked to the foot of the bed.

Her heart was thumping. Her hands were shaking. Her cheeks were wet from crying.

Still staring at the bed, she swiped her face with the side of her hand and swigged back her tears.

This time, the dream was worse.

This time, it was far more real.

Her steps unsteady, Holly stumbled over to the window and opened it. It was too early for more than a scrap of sun to be visible above the horizon. The air was still night-cool, and she closed her eyes and let the crisp breeze slap against her face, hoping the reality of the dawn would chase away the phantoms of her dream.

It didn't.

No matter how hard Holly tried to push them aside, the memories made their way into her brain. They snaked down her arms and prickled up her back. She could see it all again in her mind.

The frantic retreat through the school halls.

The desperate search for a place she would be safe.

The chilling nearness of the Presence.

But this time . . .

Holly's eyes flew open. She hugged herself, running her hands up and down her arms to try and calm the terrifying feeling of panic that stormed through her.

This time in the dream, the Presence got nearer.

She could still feel the panic that filled her when she realized the panther was right behind her. Still feel its breath hot against the back of her neck. Still smell the animal scent of the creature, primitive and savage and powerful.

Holly ran her hands through her hair and down to her neck. She kneaded the tight muscles behind her ears.

It was bad enough to dream about the Presence once, but twice in one week?

She shivered and tipped her face up, her eyes filling with tears.

"What's wrong with me?" she asked, her words unsettling the stillness of her room.

Silence was her only answer.

"Did you hear?" Tisha was talking even before she was anywhere near Holly. She called to her from across the hallway. "Everybody's talking about the dance!"

"That's nice." Holly mumbled the reply without giving it a second thought. She dug her biology book out of her locker and slammed the door shut.

After waking up from the nightmare about the panther, Holly hadn't been able to fall back to sleep. Her eyes stung. Her head hurt. Even from all the way over here, she could smell Tisha's perfume. It was so strong, it turned her stomach. She didn't really care what news Tisha or anybody else had to share this morning. All she wanted to do was to be left alone.

"They say David Kramer and Beth Hammary had a rip-roaring fight out in the parking lot after the dance." Tisha scrambled across the hallway and up to Holly. "It must be true. Tollifson's their homeroom teacher and I saw him fluttering around here this morning like a sailboat without a rudder. He must be trying to keep the peace. And Karen Johnson didn't even show up at the dance. Did you notice? After the way she talked

about her new dress all last week. And what she said
she paid for it. And—"

Tisha stood on tiptoe and peered into Holly's face.
"What's wrong with your eyes?" she asked. "They're
all red."

Holly pretended she'd forgotten something. She
turned back to her locker, dialed her combination,
and leafed through the books and papers stacked
inside. "I didn't sleep much last night," she said,
her voice ricocheting inside the metal locker. "I'm
tired and—" A wave of nausea gushed up Holly's
throat and into her mouth. She turned to Tisha. "Did
you have to put on so much perfume this morning?"

Tisha gave her a questioning look. "Perfume?" She
sniffed the air. "I don't smell any perfume."

Holly was in no mood for games. She barely had
to breathe in and she could smell the cloying scent. It
hit her in the back of the throat and sent her stomach
spinning. One hand on her locker door, she steadied
herself.

"Very funny," she said. "It's Bouquet of Summer
Roses. Your favorite. You must have ladled it on this
morning. Honestly, Tisha, it's one thing to wear a
fragrance as strong as that to the homecoming dance,
but here at school? You're going to choke everybody
in class."

"Bouquet of—?" Tisha brought her wrist to her
nose and took a sniff. "Not a trace. Smell." She held
her arm out to Holly.

Holly moved back a step. She wrinkled her nose.
"I don't need to get any closer. I can smell it from

over here. I could smell it before, when you were all the way across the corridor."

"Then you must have one heck of a nose." Tisha shook her head. "I haven't put on any Bouquet of Summer Roses since the dance Saturday night. That was two days ago, in case you forgot. And I guarantee you, I've taken a couple showers since then."

"Are you sure?"

Holly didn't need to wait for Tisha's answer. Of course Tisha was sure. Why wouldn't she be?

"I'm sorry." Holly felt far more sincere than she sounded. She sounded preoccupied and distracted, even to herself, and she apologized to Tisha as quickly as she could. "I guess I'm just tired," she said. "I woke up early and couldn't get back to sleep and—"

"No more bad dreams, I hope. No more dreams about Alex?" Tisha's brown eyes were bright with interest.

"No. No more dreams about Alex." That much was true. Holly shut her locker and turned toward her homeroom. "No dreams about anything."

"You know, David Kramer and Karen Johnson aren't the only ones everybody's talking about this morning. You guys are the talk of the school."

For a minute, Holly didn't know what Tisha was talking about.

"The dance!" Tisha poked Holly in the arm. "Everybody's talking about how you and Alex were dancing. You know, real close together."

"Were we?" Holly acted like it didn't matter in the least. She had to. If she didn't, the memory was sure to set her head spinning. All she needed to do was think back to Saturday night. She could still feel the touch of Alex's hand, still feel his arms around her.

The memory skittered through Holly like wildfire and made the way Alex picked up and left at the track last night all the more baffling.

"I'd say my plan worked pretty good." Tisha stared up into Holly's face. "Only . . . Holly . . . ? It didn't work too good, did it? I mean, it worked the way it was supposed to work, didn't it? Alex noticed you. That's what we wanted. He noticed you and you got to dance with him. That's what was supposed to happen. And you got him out of your system, right? Like me and the chocolate? Now everything can get back to normal, can't it?"

"Sure." Holly wasn't at all certain she could look right at Tisha and lie so she didn't even try. She bent down and retied her sneakers even though they didn't need it. "Everything's right as can be," she said. She smiled up at Tisha.

But everything wasn't as right as can be.

The mocking echo of her own words filled Holly's head.

Everything wasn't right.

Everything wasn't normal.

Holly didn't know why, but she was sure of one thing.

Things would never be normal again.

—————————————— 9 ——

*Not bad for a beginner. You deserve another
chance. Saturday night? Football game, wait
till the stadium's empty. Loser—that's you—buys
winner—that's me!—a pizza after.*

The note was on Holly's desk in biology when she
got there. It was written on a piece of paper torn from
a three-ring notebook. Holly rubbed her finger along
the fringe of shredded paper on one side and a ripple
of excitement zoomed around her stomach.

She glanced over to where Alex was sitting on the
other side of the biology lab. She thought he'd be
watching her, waiting to see her reaction to the note.

She should have known better.

Alex had his nose in his biology book.

Holly knew it was no use waiting for him to look
over. She read through the note one more time,
memorizing every word.

After the way Alex left the stadium so quickly last
night, she wasn't sure what to think.

Now she knew.

He was willing to give her another chance.

The thought warmed Holly's heart. After seeing

Alex run, she knew there was no way she could ever beat him. Not in this lifetime. But he was willing to give her another shot.

Or was it just an excuse to see her again?

A buzz of excitement started in Holly's head and filled her ears.

Wait till the stadium's empty.

She read the line over and over.

He wanted to see her again.

Alone.

"What's that?" Tisha dropped into the seat next to Holly and leaned over, craning her neck to see the note.

As quickly as she could, Holly folded it and stuck it in the pocket of her jeans. "Nothing."

"Nothing?" Tisha eyed Holly. She eyed Holly's pocket. "Looked like something to me. Something like a note. Not from anyone we know, is it?" Tisha raised her eyebrows. Jason was in his usual seat by the door and she looked that way. "You two planning something?"

"Only the football game Saturday night." As soon as the words were out of her mouth, Holly felt her stomach go crazy, like it did the time her dad took her out fishing on a boat. First thing this morning, Jason had asked her to Saturday's football game and she'd accepted. But if she was with Jason Saturday night, how would she get away to meet Alex?

"I'm going to the game with Zack." Tisha was too busy looking lovesick to notice that Holly had gotten very quiet. "Want to go to Gino's after?"

"Sure." Holly hoped her answer didn't sound as wishy-washy to Tisha as it did to herself. She fingered the note in her pocket.

How would she keep her date with Alex if she was already on one with Jason?

Holly didn't have time to think about it. The next second, Mr. Tollifson came flapping into the room.

Or at least she supposed it was Mr. Tollifson. All Holly could really see of him was his nose sticking out from behind the stack of books he was carrying and a long line of computer printouts that dragged behind him like a tail.

He thumped the books down on the desk.

It was Mr. Tollifson, all right. His chubby cheeks quivering, he reeled in the computer printouts. Drops of sweat shimmered like shiny beads on Mr. Tollifson's bald head. Even from the back of the room, Holly could see that his hands were shaking. "We caught something!" he said, his voice high and shrill. "We caught something in the trap!"

Holly and Tisha looked at each other. Whatever it was, it must have been something pretty spectacular. The biology teacher looked like he was about to burst with excitement.

"I have proof." Mr. Tollifson leafed through the papers on his desk and Holly saw that some of them were photographs. The glossy paper glinted in the light of the sun coming through the lab windows. "And I've run a program. Nothing elaborate." Mr. Tollifson held up the computer sheets. They dangled from his hand and trailed onto the floor.

"Feeding habits. Migratory paths. An estimate of how large the family group might be. How many adults. How many young."

"Wait a minute!" While everybody else was at the edge of their seats waiting to hear more, Jason was laughing. "Are you telling us you actually got pictures of the panther?"

"Pictures? Panther?" Mr. Tollifson's eyes got round. He scratched one finger under his nose like Holly had seen people do when they were nervous. Or lying. "Panther? Oh dear. No. I mean, what we've got here . . ." He held up one of the pictures. It showed a scared-looking animal peering out from between the bars of the cage. "We caught a raccoon!"

There was a collective sigh of disappointment from the class.

"A raccoon?" Laila's voice rose above the grumbles. "Who cares?"

"We should all care." Mr. Tollifson looked at her in amazement. "I set out to disprove this nonsense about a panther and I did . . ." Mr. Tollifson's words trailed off and he stared around the room as if he'd forgotten where he was. The next second, a shudder made his egg-shaped body tremble. He shook his head and recovered with a start.

"Ridiculous notion. All this about a panther." He waved the photograph of the raccoon. "This is far more important. Don't you see, we can study the animal's living conditions, reproductive patterns, the . . ."

Holly sank back in her seat. Like everyone else in

class, she'd been lured in by Mr. Tollifson's excitement. She shook her head, amazed at herself. Did she really think he was going to come in here and say he'd captured the Los Gatos Panther?

" . . . so you see," Mr. Tollifson was still explaining, "an animal like this"—he held up the photographs, fanned out like a deck of cards—"can really help us understand . . ."

Bored and a little disappointed, Holly copied the picture of the raccoon into her notebook. She drew the tiny nose, the bright eyes, the small, alert ears. "It's a cute little thing, isn't it?" Holly lowered her voice so only Tisha could hear her. "Look at that face, it's so sweet."

Tisha tipped her head to get a look at the drawing. "It's cute all right. But how can you see it? You don't have your glasses on."

Holly stopped, her pencil suspended over the notebook.

How could she see the photograph?

She rubbed her knuckles over her eyes and looked back up at Mr. Tollifson.

The photograph was as clear as ever.

So was everything else in the room: tonight's reading assignment on the blackboard, the stars and stripes in the flag that hung over the desk, every leaf of every tree outside the lab windows.

Holly knew she should have been thrilled and yet . . .

Grabbing her glasses out of her purse, she settled them on the end of her nose.

She looked at Mr. Tollifson over the frames.

She could see him perfectly. Every bead of sweat on his forehead. Every hair—what he had left of them—on his head.

She pushed the glasses up her nose and looked at Mr. Tollifson through the lenses.

Everything was blurry. As blurry as it used to be when she looked at things without her glasses.

Holly pulled the glasses off and tossed them back in her purse.

She gave Tisha a one-sided smile that said she didn't understand what was going on, either.

" . . . so you see, we've proven the value of the trap." From up at the front of the room, Mr. Tollifson was still rambling on. "I'll bait the trap again and we'll see what we catch next. In the meantime, if you'll open your books to Chapter Three . . ."

"Is it true you used raw meat to bait the trap?"

Holly looked up at the sound of Alex's voice.

He was sitting back in his seat, his arms crossed over his chest, his voice sharp and clear, as if he was issuing a challenge.

Mr. Tollifson seemed caught by surprise. "Raw meat? Well, yes . . ." He thumbed through the photographs until he found the one he wanted. It showed Mr. Tollifson himself setting a large portion of very raw and very disgusting-looking meat in front of the open door of the cage. "I prepared the camera myself last night," he said. "It was on a timer. Set to snap a picture every few minutes. Here I am baiting the trap. I—"

"Do raccoons eat raw steak?"

Again, the question was from Alex.

Mr. Tollifson ran one finger around the inside of his collar. "Raccoons eat anything," he said. "They are scavengers for the most part and—"

"And would they eat raw steak? I mean, that much raw steak?"

Mr. Tollifson cleared his throat. "What exactly are you suggesting, Mr. Sarandon?"

"Me?" Holly couldn't help but notice how the muscles in Alex's back and arms rippled as he shifted in his seat. "I'm not suggesting anything. You know biology better than any of us do. It just seems funny that an animal as small as that . . ." He motioned toward the photograph of the raccoon. "Could eat so much in one night. It seems like something a bigger animal would eat. A lot bigger animal."

"Bigger?" Mr. Tollifson's voice trailed away. He looked around the classroom, his eyes wide, his top lip glistening with sweat. "Bigger . . ." He rummaged through the photographs on his desk. "Yes . . . Well . . . This little fellow obviously has quite a big appetite." Mr. Tollifson's laugh was as strained as the look on his face. "And that brings us to Chapter Three . . ."

Tisha dropped her pencil so she could lean over and whisper to Holly. "It doesn't bring us to Chapter Three at all. Chapter Three is about starfish." She indicated Mr. Tollifson with a lift of her eyebrows. "What do you suppose is bugging him?"

Holly shook her head and opened her book to Chapter Three. She didn't know what was wrong with Mr. Tollifson, but it obviously was something. He looked as jumpy as a kid on his way to the doctor for a flu shot.

It didn't help his class one bit. His lecture was disjointed. His examples didn't make a bit of sense. His homework assignment was nearly impossible.

Holly found her attention roaming.

Directly over to Alex Sarandon.

He was taking notes, his pen gliding over the paper. Holly could picture his writing, the same straight, dark writing in her note.

Slipping the note out of her pocket, Holly smoothed it open between the pages of her biology book.

This Saturday? The loser buys the winner a pizza.

The words were so plain. So tempting.

She would meet Alex and—

"Ms. Callison?"

Holly's head shot up when she realized Mr. Tollifson was calling her name.

He put his hands behind his back and rocked up on the balls of his feet. "If you were listening instead of reading notes, Ms. Callison, perhaps you would have heard my question."

Holly felt her face get as red as her hair.

Mr. Tollifson stared down at her. "Stop up at my desk after class." He didn't wait for her to answer. He knew she had no choice. Mr. Tollifson pivoted around and found a new victim.

"Ah, Mr. Van Kirk . . . you think this is amusing? Then let's see how funny you think it is to discuss the anatomy of a starfish."

Holly felt sorry for Jason. He was taking the brunt of Mr. Tollifson's anger. But Jason didn't seem to mind. He answered every one of Tollifson's questions and answered them right. When he was done, he winked at Holly.

Grateful, Holly smiled over at him. It was a smile that didn't last long.

Just thinking about Saturday night made Holly feel guilty.

Her smile faded at the same time she found her gaze moving from Jason to Alex. Her mind was wandering along with it. Right back to last night.

In spite of herself, Holly couldn't forget how it felt to be with Alex. How she tingled when he touched her. How her knees turned to Jell-O and her palms got itchy and her heart thumped like a jackhammer when he put his lips close to hers and whispered, "Oh, Holly."

Holly shook her shoulders to get rid of the thought before she melted into a puddle of mush right here in biology.

That was enough to help her make up her mind.

She wasn't sure how she'd arrange it.

She wasn't sure how she'd get rid of Jason after the football game.

But she would.

She promised herself that.

She was going to meet Alex on Saturday night no matter what.

Even if it killed her.

• • •

Mr. Tollifson didn't look at Holly. He was too busy stacking his photographs into a pile.

But he knew she was there. Holly could tell because he was making little clicking noises with his tongue, noises that made it clear he hadn't forgotten the day that Holly's notebook skittered onto the floor in the middle of one of his lectures.

"First you disrupt my class," Mr. Tollifson said. "Now this." With a jiggle of his shoulders, he tapped the pile of photographs against his desktop. "You really must learn to control yourself, Ms. Callison. You cannot answer my questions if you're busy reading notes. You must learn to pay attention."

"Yes, Mr. Tollifson, I—"

"You are disturbing my class." Mr. Tollifson arranged the pages of computer printouts. "I just can't allow that."

"No, Mr. Tollifson, I—"

"You won't have time to think about what sort of trouble you're going to cause the rest of the week. You'll be too busy writing a five-hundred-word essay on the digestive system of a starfish. It's due Friday."

"Yes, Mr. Tollifson, I—"

Mr. Tollifson wasn't even listening.

He grabbed his books and papers, perched the photographs on top of the pile and dashed out of the room.

He was already out the door when Holly noticed he'd left one photograph behind. She picked it up and started out the door after him.

"Mr. Tollif—"

The name froze on Holly's lips.

She stared down at the photo in her hands. This wasn't one of the pictures Mr. Tollifson had shown the class. This photo was blurry, crooked, as if the camera had been knocked over and the picture snapped just before it hit the ground. The light wasn't very good, either. The picture was a mishmash of light and dark shadows.

Holly tipped the picture toward the windows to get a better look at it.

Up in the left-hand corner, she could make out what she supposed was the bottom edge of the trap. The rest of the picture showed the ground in front of it.

No wonder Mr. Tollifson hadn't shown them this photograph. It was a disaster. Holly held the picture away from her, her arms straight, her eyes squeezed nearly shut.

The little bit of distance brought the whole thing into focus.

Holly leaned back against Mr. Tollifson's desk and stared at the photograph in her hands. Her mind whirled. Her ears filled with the noise of her blood rushing through her veins.

It was the picture of an animal pawprint.

A large pawprint.

The pawprint of a cat.

"No wonder Tollifson was so excited all through class," Holly said under her breath. "It sure wasn't about any old raccoon."

Mr. Tollifson had found something a lot more interesting than a raccoon. He'd found proof of the existence of the Los Gatos Panther.

Holly looked at the door where Mr. Tollifson had just gone out.

She wondered how much else he knew that he was keeping to himself.

Even as she thrashed beneath her blankets, Holly knew it was a dream. A dream that contained the images of all the disturbing things she'd seen today in biology.

Still, she couldn't stop it.

Helpless, she was sucked into the nightmare. She found herself outside the door of the biology room, looking down at the floor, at the muddy pawprint of a gigantic cat and the mound of bloody meat stacked near the door.

Holly didn't have to turn around to know the Panther was right behind her. Just like last night. She could feel the big cat there, its breath hot against the backs of her legs.

It wanted the meat.

How Holly knew it, she wasn't sure. But something told her she was right. The panther wanted the meat, and if he got it, he would be more powerful than ever. Too powerful to fight. Too powerful to get away from.

Even though her stomach did flip-flops every time she looked at it, Holly reached for the steak. It was cold. It was slick and wet with blood. She jerked her hands back, stretched them out again. Lifted the meat into her arms.

As if it were alive, the formless lump slipped and slid until she settled it against her chest.

Holly squeezed her eyes shut and swallowed the sour taste in her mouth.

She had to keep the meat away from the panther. She couldn't let him have it.

The next thing she knew, Holly was running through the halls, the steak held up close to her body like a baby. The meat was ruining her favorite nightgown, leaving a hideous mark that soaked through to her skin and stained it red. The blood spattered on her face and dotted her arms. It dripped on the floor, leaving a trail for the panther to follow.

Holly dodged into the art corridor and down the stairs that led to the first-floor hallway.

The scent of the blood rose up to her from the bundle in her arms. It turned her stomach at the same time it made her mouth water and her eyeteeth tingle. Holly ran her tongue over her teeth and turned her face away. The smell was making her dizzy.

Propping the meat in the crook of her left arm, Holly steadied herself, her right hand against the hand-rail.

That's when she heard it. A noise at the top of the stairs. A low, steady growl that echoed against the walls and filled her ears and sent her heart into her throat.

Holly looked over her shoulder.

There was no sign of the panther, but she knew he

was there. He was waiting in the shadows. Waiting for the meat.

There was only one thing to do.

Holly sat down on the bottom step. She picked up the first piece of meat and began to eat.

10

Holly's eyes flew open.

Her hands were cold. Her nightgown was soaked.

She wasn't in her bedroom.

She passed one hand over her eyes. Her hands felt wet, too, and she brushed them against each other, trying to get rid of whatever it was that made them so cold and sticky.

After a moment, the clock on the stove came into focus. Four in the morning.

Holly shook her head, trying to clear away the cobwebs.

The rest of the house was dark and quiet. From upstairs, she could hear her dad's steady snores and her mom turning over in bed, punching her pillow and groaning in her sleep.

But Holly was in the kitchen. And it was four o'clock in the morning.

There was an odd taste in her mouth, kind of like metal. It stuck at the back of her throat and, even when she swallowed, it wouldn't go away. Holly ran her tongue over her teeth and lips to try to get rid of it. That didn't work, either. For a second, she thought she'd get up and get a glass of water, but her legs

ached like she'd just run for miles and miles and she
forgot about the water. She slumped in her chair.

She was sitting at the kitchen table. Across the
room, the refrigerator door was standing open. In the
pool of light made by the single bulb, she could see
that the drawers of the refrigerator were pulled out.
The bottles and containers her mom usually kept in
such neat order on the shelves were laying every
which way as if someone had rummaged through
looking for something. On the floor, the remains of
some kind of plastic packaging winked at her.

Holly held out her hands to the light.

They were slick and dark and she rubbed them
against her nightgown. It was already spotted with
something wet. Something dark. Something red.

Holly spun in her chair to face the light.

Her nightgown was dotted with blood. The same
blood that speckled her hands and felt wet and sticky
on her face.

Holly's throat tightened around every breath. Her
heart beat so hard, it hurt.

She didn't want to turn toward the table, but she
knew she had to. She had to see.

Holly squeezed her eyes closed and swung around
in the chair.

"Open your eyes," she ordered herself, her voice
small and scared in the dark. "Open your eyes and
find out for sure. You've got to before you wake up
Mom and Dad."

She didn't have to open them far.

Holly was already looking down at the table, and before her eyes were all the way open, she saw what was on it.

A raw steak. Half-eaten.

Holly clamped her hands to her mouth. It was the only way she could stop her scream.

The rest of the week was a blur.

Holly went to school every day. She went to all her classes. She even managed to do the essay on starfish for Mr. Tollifson.

She wasn't sure how, except that she must have had some sort of automatic pilot, a self-preservation device that allowed her to go through the week like a robot, doing what she needed to do. Because she didn't want them to suspect anything, she was as cheerful as could be with Mom and Dad. She gossiped with Tisha and flirted with Jason and watched Alex like she always did.

She wondered what they would say if they knew she was crazy.

Holly winced. She still wasn't used to the idea.

But there wasn't any other answer, was there?

For the thousandth time she asked herself the question. For the thousandth time, she came up with the same answer.

She was crazy.

Crazy enough so that she had to lock her bedroom door each night to keep herself from roaming the house.

Crazy enough to dream about the panther every time she fell asleep.

Crazy enough to be here in the empty stadium, waiting for Alex.

Holly took off her jacket and tossed it over the nearest railing. She let her gaze wander to where the oval track disappeared into the pitch-black shadows.

She hadn't felt like running for days and even if she had, she was sure she never would have had the energy. Maybe this would help.

Maybe the feel of the air rushing past her face would clear her head and make her think better. Maybe it would just exhaust her and make her sleep. Sleep without dreaming.

"How'd you like the game?"

Alex came up behind her and slipped one arm around her shoulders.

Holly didn't even jump. By now, she was used to him appearing from out of nowhere. She didn't melt at his touch, either. Not this time. She was too exhausted to care.

"You did good." She gave Alex a weak smile, the only kind she could seem to manage lately. "We won."

It was a dumb thing to say. Of course he knew they had won. Alex was the star of the game.

Sure that he was looking at her like she was stupid and just as sure she didn't want to see the look, Holly pulled away. She did a few knee bends.

Alex was wearing a white T-shirt and dark workout shorts. He had a red sweater in one hand. He slung it over one shoulder and leaned against the railing. "You really want to race?" he asked.

Holly snapped back at him, "If you didn't think I wanted to race, why did you ask me here?"

Alex obviously wasn't prepared for her show of temper. He pursed his lips and gave a silent whistle. Propelling himself from the railing, he dropped his sweater on the bottom bleacher and crossed the distance between them, his movements even and graceful, his eyes fixed on Holly.

"I asked you here so I could see you again," he said. He cupped Holly's chin in his hand and held her face steady. She had no choice but to look at him. "I asked you here because I wanted to be with you."

A week ago, his words would have sent her streaking up to the sky like a Fourth of July rocket. Today, they only made Holly feel worse.

"You don't want to see me." She moved away. Maybe it was her exhaustion that made her feel so daring, maybe it was just another symptom of how crazy she really was, but she didn't feel like playing games. Not anymore.

"If you really wanted to see me, you wouldn't ask me to meet you in the middle of the night when no one was around." Carefully, she watched Alex's face to catch his reaction. There wasn't one. He was just looking at her, listening.

His lack of response only made Holly madder. "If you really wanted to see me," she said, "you'd just ask me out like any normal guy would. And I'd say 'yes,' and then I wouldn't have to sneak around and lie to Jason and—"

"Ah! That's it!" Alex's face split with a grin. "Feeling guilty about Boy Jason, are you? How'd you manage to get away from him this evening?"

It wasn't something she felt good about.

Holly let out a long sigh. "I told him I had a headache. I asked him to take me home right after the game. And when he did—"

"When he did, you slipped right out the back door and came over here." Alex's eyes lit with the kind of sparkle Holly had seen in her parents' eyes when she did something that made them proud. "You lied to the boy? Just for me? That is a scheme worthy of Laila herself. And no one is sneakier than Laila."

"Thanks a lot." Holly glared at him.

Alex threw his hands in the air. "What do you want from me?" he asked.

Holly looked over to where Alex stood, his hair still damp from his after-game shower, a curl of it hanging over his forehead like a dark question mark against his skin.

What did she want from him?

Holly didn't know. All she knew was that Alex was perfect. He was everything she had ever wanted in a boyfriend. And she didn't want him to know she was crazy.

She wanted to forget all about that herself.

And the only way she could think to do that was to run, to run until she outpaced her worries and left them far behind. To run until she fell over, so exhausted she couldn't possibly dream about the panther.

Holly raised her chin. "What I really want," she said, "is to beat you around this track. You want to get started?"

She didn't wait for Alex to answer. Without another look at him, she jogged over to the starting line and bent one knee to the ground.

He didn't say a word till he was down on one knee beside her. "Once around?"

"Once around," she answered. "On my count of three."

This time, Alex got off the starting line first. Holly wasn't surprised. Last time, he'd tried to fool her into thinking she actually had a chance to win. This time, there was no need for him to try to trick her. He knew he was going to win. She knew he was going to win. There was no use pretending.

Maybe it only proved how crazy she really was, but Holly didn't care.

She paced herself around the track, and when she saw Alex pull out far ahead just like he did last time, she ran as fast as she could.

She pushed herself hard.

Harder.

Before she knew it, she was right behind Alex.

Holly dragged in a deep breath of air.

Harder.

The air rushed against Holly's face. The night streamed past her. Holly gave herself to the feeling of flying.

Her exhaustion lifted. Her worries flew away with it. She didn't feel the tightness in her chest, the soreness in her legs, the pounding of her blood in her temples. She didn't feel anything.

She was no more than a shadow that slipped through the darkness, no more than a whisper on the wind, a streak of movement that merged with the night and the wind and the dark.

She passed Alex up as if he were standing still.

The rest of the race went by in a fog.

Holly vaguely remembered zooming past the goal-posts at the end of the football field. She barely caught sight of the yard-line markers, stark and white against the playing field. She didn't see Alex again. He never caught up.

Holly dashed across the finish line and slowed down to a jog. She went ten yards or so around the track, turned around, trotted back the other way. She wasn't winded. She wasn't tired. Her legs didn't ache the way they usually did after a race.

Her spine arrow-straight, her shoulders back, she was waiting for Alex when he crossed the finish line.

"Looks like you owe me a pizza." Holly couldn't help herself. She was smiling. Smiling for the first time in a week.

Alex pulled up beside Holly. He shook his head, trying to figure out what happened. "What the—?"

Holly couldn't help herself. She started to laugh.

"How'd you do that?" Alex didn't look nearly as cool, calm and collected as he had after their last race. His hair was sticking up at funny angles all over his head and he was breathing hard, hard enough that his chest strained against his sweat-soaked T-shirt.

Holly only laughed harder. Funny, she'd never taken Alex for the type who was a sore loser. Yet he looked . . .

Holly's laugh settled into a wide smile as she tried to analyze the expression that tugged down the corners of Alex's mouth and crinkled around his eyes.

He didn't look as angry as he looked dazed. He didn't look as dazed as he did mystified. He clamped one hand down on her arm. "Holly, I asked how you did that?"

"I outran you, plain and simple." Smoothly, Holly pulled away from his grip. The push of adrenaline that had made her fast enough to win the race had gone to her head. She felt dizzy. Cocky. Reckless.

"And you owe me a pizza." She tapped one finger on Alex's chin and let it rest there, just a fraction of an inch from his lips. "Remember? The loser—that's you—" She trailed her finger down his chin to his neck, down his neck to his chest, and jabbed gently at the rock-hard muscles of his stomach. "Buys the winner—that's me—" She gave him her most dazzling smile. "A pizza."

"I remember." Alex was breathing harder than ever, and Holly was sure it had nothing to do with the race. His pupils were so large, his eyes looked as dark as the night sky above them. They reflected the lights of the signs over the stadium exits, small pinpoints of red floating in a sea of glassy black.

As quick as a cat, he snatched up Holly's hand

and held it against his heart. "Yes, I do owe you a pizza," he said. He was smiling now, too, smiling and leaning nearer, near enough to slide his other arm around Holly's waist and settle his hand against the small of her back. "And you owe me some answers. Come on." He nudged her toward the exit. "I want to know all about you."

Holly leaned her head back against Alex's shoulder. "Mmm." The sound came from deep in her throat, a sound of contentment and satisfaction. "That would be nice," she purred. "Pizza and conversation and . . ."

She was just as quick as Alex was.

Before he even knew what was happening, she was out of his arms and heading for the exit at a trot. "Maybe some other night," she called to him over her shoulder. "I'm not very hungry."

It was just like the first dream.

She was back in the library.

There was an open book on the table in front of Holly. She slammed it shut. Stretching her arms over her head, she pushed back her chair. It scraped against the wooden floor, the sound deafening in the silence of the deserted school building.

It didn't matter, she told herself. There was no use trying to be quiet. The panther knew she was here. He knew everything about her.

A gurgle of strangled laughter rose up from Holly's throat. She couldn't seem to help herself. There was no use trying to be quiet, just as there was no use trying to run away.

She couldn't fool him. She couldn't hide from him.

The thought settled in Holly's stomach like a block of ice. It froze her blood.

The panther knew she dreamed of him every night, and the knowledge made him powerful. He knew she thought about him even when she was awake. Somehow, Holly was sure he knew it.

The panther knew she ate raw meat and licked the blood from her lips.

Holly shook away the memory.

Rising from her chair, she drew in a deep breath. The aromas of the empty school building hung in the air like laundry on a line: messy lockers and forgotten lunch bags, smelly sneakers from the gym, and paint from the art rooms, and the biting odor of chemicals coming from the labs on the floor below.

Holly's nostrils flared and she drew in another breath.

There was another smell mingled with them all, one that made her feel like she had just gotten off a roller coaster. Like her feet weren't quite touching the floor, and her head was whirling, and her stomach was flopping around like a freshly caught fish.

The smell was strange, tantalizing, and Holly found herself smiling and turning toward the door, prepared to go in search of its source.

It was the smell of fear.

She didn't care if the panther was here. She would find the source of the smell. She had to. And if the panther found her first?

Holly's smile widened and a hum of excitement

vibrated through her chest and in her throat.

Let him try.

There was something about teasing him that appealed to her tonight, just like it did when she dared to tease Alex after the race. There was something about tempting fate that sent a tickle of excitement up her spine and into her brain. Something about flirting with danger that suddenly interested her far more than running from it.

Her footsteps completely silent, her passing no more than a flicker in the shadows, Holly slipped through the door and down the nearest stairway. She got as far as the second-floor landing and stopped.

There was a light on in the biology room. It wasn't bright, but it hurt her eyes. Curious to find out what was going on, Holly started for the room.

Before she could get there, the door snapped open and a girl came into the corridor. The girl's back was to her; Holly couldn't see her face. She was wearing dark-colored pants and a denim shirt, like the one Tisha sometimes wore, the one Holly liked so much she'd gone out and bought one just like it.

But this wasn't Tisha. The girl was too tall. There were no lights on in the corridor, but her hair looked lighter than Tisha's. It was longer and pulled back in a ponytail and away from the girl's neck.

Holly raised her head and sniffed the air.

This was where the smell of fear was coming from, she realized. From this girl.

The girl was afraid. Very afraid.

Afraid of Holly.

The knowledge tore through Holly's veins. It made her blood feel hot and her mouth water.

Holly shifted her gaze from the back of the girl's hair to the strip of bare skin that showed between her ponytail and her collar. Funny, she thought, she had never noticed anyone's neck before, not like this. She had never noticed how the light played against the ripple of the spine just below the skin, or how you could see a pulse beating just behind the ear.

Holly noticed it now. And it made her hungry.

Slowly, slipping in and out of the shadows, Holly followed the girl. Down the science corridor, past the art rooms, down the stairs to the first-floor hallway. The girl went into the newspaper office and Holly settled herself in the shadows outside the door, beneath the painting of the Los Gatos Panther.

Tonight, the panther was right where he belonged. Holly looked up at the magnificent animal on the wall. His claws glistened with the reflected light of the exit signs, his fur was sleek and beautiful. His teeth shone with saliva and blood. His eyes gleamed.

That's when Holly knew.

She looked down at herself, at the sleek coat of black fur, the graceful, muscular legs, the claws, so quick they could snatch a bird out of the air, so powerful, they could tear apart an animal twice her size with a single swipe.

A tremor fluttered around Holly's mouth, an expression that was almost a smile.

She knew she was one with the panther.

At a sound from the newspaper office, she rose to

her feet and moved across the corridor, one silent step at a time. When the girl came out of the newspaper office, she was waiting for her.

The muscles of her back legs were strong and powerful. Holly pounced. Her claws out, she swiped them across the girl's chest. She heard the fabric of the denim shirt tear right before she landed on the girl, her mouth open, her fangs bared.

That's when she realized who it was.

It was Holly Callison.

Holly's own face came into focus only inches away. It was like looking in a mirror and seeing a distorted reflection of herself, a Holly whose face was transformed by terror. Her hazel eyes were wide, her mouth was open in a scream, tears streamed down her cheeks.

A flash of pity stormed through Holly when she looked at the girl, a flash that lasted no longer than a second. She could not help herself, even if she wanted to. It was her nature to do what she was doing, her nature, the nature of a panther. She raised one powerful paw above Holly Callison's throat, ready for the kill.

As quickly as her own terrified face came into focus, a mist covered Holly's eyes.

The scene changed.

A cool breeze ruffled along her back. Holly's feet sunk into what felt like grass, damp with morning dew.

The dream fog cleared and Holly was in Panther Hollow.

The Holly Callison of the dream was gone. In her place was Mr. Tollifson.

The biology teacher lay on the ground beneath the weight of the panther. His mouth opened and closed and a series of pitiful, frightened sounds came from him, like the cries of a wounded animal. He twisted beneath Holly's weight, struggling, fighting for his life. With his fists, he beat against her, his punches no more than an annoyance to her, like the irritating sting of a mosquito.

Holly watched a tiny muscle twitch at the base of Mr. Tollifson's neck. Her mouth watered. Her brain spun out of control.

Without another second's hesitation, she lowered her mouth and ripped open Mr. Tollifson's throat.

11

This time, it took longer for Holly to wake up.

She didn't bolt up in bed like she usually did at the end of the nightmare. Her eyes fluttered open and it took a minute or two before they adjusted to the bright morning sunlight and the way it glanced off the white-and-gold ceiling fan above her bed.

She was awake. She knew she was. She could see the birds flitting from branch to branch in the tree outside her window. She could smell the aroma of fresh-brewed coffee coming from the kitchen downstairs. She could hear the steady bubble of the shower in the bathroom down the hall and her dad's deep baritone voice singing a song that had something to do with the moon in June.

But her brain still felt like it was in the ozone.

Holly scoured her hands over her face and propped herself up on her elbows. Her head felt as heavy as her brain, and she dropped back down on her pillow. Slowly, the memories of her dream came into focus, washing over her like a wave of cold water: the girl with Holly's face, the horrifying feeling of not being stalked by the panther, but *being* the panther, the terrified look on Mr. Tollifson's face when she drove her fangs into his neck.

The memory made Holly's stomach queasy. She turned over on her side and groaned. Her arms ached, her head hurt, and there was an odd, metallic sort of taste in her mouth that reminded her of the flavor of the raw steak she'd eaten a week ago.

Holly peeked over the edge of the blankets.

There was no sign of meat anywhere in the room. No sign that she'd gone to the kitchen anytime during the night.

The running shorts and T-shirt she'd worn for her race against Alex were still where she had left them last night, right up against the bedroom door. Her running shoes were with them.

Holly stretched out her legs and breathed a sigh of relief.

The feeling vanished when she realized there was something at the foot of her bed.

Holly squeezed her eyes shut and shifted beneath the blankets. There was something there, all right.

She wiggled her toes.

It wasn't something heavy, just something that didn't belong there. Something she was certain she hadn't left on the bed last night.

Holly sat up.

There were clothes piled at the foot of her bed, clothes she could have sworn she didn't leave there. They weren't clean clothes; her mom always left those folded on the rocking chair in the corner. These clothes were worn, dirty, and Holly rose to her knees and poked at the lumpy pile.

Her good sneakers were on top.

Holly picked up one shoe. There was mud all over the bottom of it, mud that was still wet. The other shoe was caked with mud, too, the same mud that was smeared all over the white quilt she used as a bedspread.

Holly tossed the shoes onto the floor. Below them on the pile were her new black jeans, the ones mom had bought her to replace the jeans she'd ruined the night of the homecoming bonfire. Holly picked up the pants. Both knees were damp. There was mud caked around the ankles. She tossed them on top of her sneakers and stared down at what was left on her bedspread.

It was a denim shirt. Her new denim shirt. The one she bought because she liked the way Tisha's looked. The one she was sure she had never worn.

The shirt was dirty, too. Dirty and wrinkled. But it wasn't the dirt that sent Holly's heart into her throat.

It was the three slits across the front of the shirt.

The ones that looked like they'd been made by the claws of an enormous cat.

Holly pushed open the screen door and stepped out onto the porch. It was cool for October, cooler than it would have been in Cleveland this time of the year, and she snapped the front door closed behind her. She tugged her green sweatshirt jacket tighter around her body and looked down the length of the porch that went along the front of the house.

Jason was waiting for her on the swing at the far end of the porch, munching on a candy bar.

When he saw her, Jason gulped down a mouthful of candy and stuck the rest of the half-eaten candy bar into his pocket. He popped out of the swing so quickly, it knocked against the backs of his legs, but Jason didn't seem to care. He just stood there, his hands in the pockets of his navy blue windbreaker.

"Hope I'm not bothering you or anything," Jason said. He fixed his gaze directly over Holly's left shoulder and kept it there, his look steadier than his voice.

"I guess your mom told you I came by this morning. Early. She said you weren't out of bed yet or maybe you were but you just weren't out of your room. She said I should come back later so . . ." Jason shrugged his broad shoulders. "Here I am."

Holly knew she should say something. Anything. She knew she should tell Jason to sit back down and go sit next to him. But she didn't. She just stood there, her arms wrapped around herself to keep from shivering.

Jason took a step forward and held out one hand. He glanced at the swing. "Maybe we'd both be more comfortable if we'd sit down," he suggested.

Holly ignored his outstretched hand. She crossed the porch and perched on the edge of the porch railing.

Even though he tried not to show it, Jason's face registered his disappointment. He plunked down on the swing. He didn't rock. He wedged his worn sneakers against the painted floor so he couldn't move, leaned forward, and propped his elbows on his knees.

"Want to talk about it?" he asked.

Holly wanted to answer, but the words just didn't

seem to be able to make their way past the painful ball of emotion jammed inside her throat. She
looked away.

"Holly?" Jason tried again. His voice was quieter,
more intense.

Holly knew there was a hurt look in Jason's eyes
and she didn't want to see it. But something about his
voice made her turn to him.

"Look!" Jason gave her a very good imitation of
a smile and turning his head, he pointed to his ears.
"Two ears. No waiting. I'll sit here all day and listen
if you'll just talk." When he didn't get a response
from Holly, his smile faded and the light in his eyes
dimmed.

Holly couldn't stand to see him look so miserable.
Not because of her. She looked down at the porch
floor and prayed that the hair that fell over her eyes
covered her face and hid her tears.

She heard the porch swing squeak and saw the toes
of Jason's shoes come into her line of vision. "I know
about you and Alex," Jason said. He tried to sound
brave but Holly couldn't miss the underlying note of
sadness in his voice, as if he had to force himself to
speak.

"I know you danced together at homecoming and
that's okay with me," he said. "I mean, it was just a
dance, right? And, big deal, it doesn't mean anything
just to dance with somebody. And . . ." Jason's words
faded away. He cleared his throat.

"I mean if that's what's bugging you, don't let it.
I'm not mad or anything. I couldn't be mad at you.

Only . . . Holly? If it's something else . . . If it's you and me and you don't think it's working and you'd rather be with Alex, well, heck . . ." Jason made a clicking noise with his tongue.

"I guess I could understand that, too," he said on the tail end of a sigh. "I wouldn't like it, but I'd understand it. Alex is a great guy and every girl in school thinks he's gorgeous. If you two are . . . well, if you're interested in each other, I—"

"This doesn't have anything to do with Alex." Holly looked up in time to see some of the worry fade from Jason's expression. As quickly as the look vanished, it was back again. His eyes filled with unbearable tenderness, he bent down on one knee. He brushed the hair out of Holly's eyes and gently tucked it behind her ear.

"Then are you sick or something?" Jason placed one hand against her forehead. Satisfied she wasn't burning with fever, he sat back on his heels and took one of Holly's hands in his.

"You look like you're on the wrong end of a bad night," he said without a trace of teasing in his voice. "You have dark circles under your eyes and your cheeks are the color of vanilla ice cream. You've been so quiet the last week or so and then, last night, when you wanted to come home right after the game, I figured there was something really wrong. If there's anything I can do, Holly, you know all you have to do is ask. Just tell me what's wrong. What is it you want?"

Holly blinked back her tears.

It was the second time in twenty-four hours that someone had asked her the same question. Last night when Alex asked her, she wasn't sure what to answer. But now she knew. She knew exactly what she wanted.

She wanted someone to talk to. Someone who could tell her why the panther stalked her every night and, why last night, *she* was the one doing the stalking. She wanted someone to explain how her clothes could get muddy when she was sure she hadn't worn them, someone who could give her some reasonable, logical explanation as to why her shirt was torn, just like the shirt of the Holly in her dream.

She wanted someone who would listen to her and tell her she wasn't crazy. She wanted someone who would tell her everything was going to be all right.

Was Jason that someone?

Holly looked into Jason's eyes and saw the answer. She squeezed his hand. "It's a dream," she said, her words wavering on the tears that suddenly filled her voice. "A dream I've been having since we moved here. I—"

Before Holly had a chance to say any more, Tisha came bounding up the front steps.

She looked like one of those zombies in the old movies, her eyes wide and staring, her skin the color of ashes.

"Holy—!" Jason took one look at Tisha and jumped up. He grabbed Tisha by the shoulders and steered her toward the swing.

"Tisha?" Jason stooped over and tried to capture

Tisha's blank gaze. "Tisha?"

But Tisha didn't say anything. She just sat there and stared at them and Holly could see that she had been crying. Tisha's cheeks were streaked with tears. Her eyes were red. Her lower lip quivered. Finally, like she'd just woken up from a nightmare, she shook her head and looked around. "You guys haven't heard?" Tisha asked.

When neither Jason nor Holly answered, Tisha scooted forward. The swing bucked and swayed. Tisha braced herself, her arms stiff, her palms against the wooden seat, and waited until it settled down. When it finally did, her face looked a little green.

Pressing her fist to her mouth, Tisha took a few deep breaths. Her eyes filled with tears and she looked up at the ceiling. "Jeez! Why do I have to be the TNN?" Tisha wailed. "Why do I have to know everything before everybody else does? Why do I have to be the one to tell you guys?"

She sniffed and ran her hands over her cheeks. "It's Mr. Tollifson," Tisha said. "He's . . . he's dead."

The words didn't register in Holly's brain. They settled in her gut. Cold, like a claw of fear. Painful, like the sharp stab of a knife. They sunk into her stomach and made it turn upside down.

Even before Tisha could go on with her story, Holly knew what she would say.

"They're going to make the announcement to the whole school tomorrow," Tisha said between sobs, "but I don't think they're going to tell everything. Grammy found out from Linda Roles. You know, the girl at the library who's dating that new deputy in the sheriff's department. He said . . ." Tisha gulped. "He said Tollifson must have been checking the trap. They found him up at Panther Hollow."

Panther Hollow.

The words echoed in Holly's ears.

Panther Hollow where the cold breeze in her dream flowed along her back and the ground felt soft beneath her feet, muddy with the same mud that was caked on her sneakers.

"That's not the worst of it." Tisha's voice was wobbly. She looked right at Holly. "They said it looked like Tollifson had been attacked by an animal. A big animal. Oh, Holly! I just knew something like this was going to happen. Why wouldn't anyone listen to me when I warned them about Panther Hollow?"

Even with Tisha staring right at her, Holly couldn't react. She felt like a block of stone.

It seemed Jason was the only one levelheaded enough to do anything. He put his arm around Tisha's shoulders. "It's okay, Little Bit. Just 'cause they found Tollifson dead up at the Hollow doesn't mean a thing. He was pretty old. Heck, he must have been forty-five. And he was out of shape. The long climb up there might have—"

"Is that why his throat was ripped open?" Tisha twisted around to face Jason, her voice high and shrill. "His whole throat, Jason. All of it. Gone. Just like a wild animal would do. And that's not all. Remember what Alex said? At the homecoming bonfire, remember what he said about panthers? He said they were selfish hunters. He said they were the only animals that hauled their kill up to the branches of a tree to keep any other animals from getting at it." Tisha turned frenzied eyes on Holly.

"That's where they found Mr. Tollifson. His body was dragged up into the branches of a tree."

It took a long time before Tisha calmed down enough for Jason to take her home. While he was gone, Holly sat on the porch and stared off into space listening to Tisha's chilling news play and replay itself in her mind.

His throat torn open.

His body dragged up into the branches of a tree.

Holly shuddered.

Even before Tisha had told them the whole story about Mr. Tollifson, Holly knew what she would say. She knew Tisha would say Mr. Tollifson was killed by a wild animal. She knew Tisha would tell them his throat was torn open.

Holly ran her tongue over her lips.

Of course she knew. She could still taste Mr. Tollifson's blood.

"Pretty awful stuff, huh?"

Sometime while Holly was lost in thought, Jason came back. He rested one hand on her shoulder and settled himself on the porch railing next to her.

"Tisha's pretty shook up," Jason said. "I talked to her grandma. Told her I thought maybe Tisha shouldn't be left alone. I guess it's all we can do for her. I guess it's all anybody can do."

Holly felt Jason slide one arm around her. "And how are you doing?" he asked.

Holly turned her face away so Jason couldn't see the horror in her eyes.

"Yeah, me, too." Jason pulled her against his shoulder. His voice was quiet, thoughtful. "I don't know what to think. And I'm not sure what to feel. I feel sorry for Tollifson, sure. Who wouldn't? But I feel confused, too. All that stuff about the panther, it can't be true. But . . ." The logic of Jason's argument dissolved in light of the facts. As if to hide his uneasiness, he gave Holly a quick hug.

"I'm sorry. This isn't helping you at all." Jason moved back far enough so he could look at her. "You were already upset about something before all this happened. It's unfair to heap any more of it on you." He took Holly's hand in his and tipped his head, trying to get a look at her face. "Go ahead, Holly, tell me what's been bothering you. Maybe talking about something else will take both our minds off Tollifson. And don't worry, I know that the two of us, together, we can work it out."

Holly relaxed against Jason's shoulder and tilted her head up to look into his eyes. There was something soothing and hypnotic about his voice, something that called to the Holly she'd been when they first met all those weeks ago, something that wrapped itself around her heart and warmed her insides like hot chocolate on a cold morning.

Jason's eyes looked blue as sapphires in the late-afternoon light. His hair shone like gold. The dimple in his chin was shadowed and dusted with a few short, golden whiskers that made him look more mature and cuter all at the same time.

Jason was fine and smart and tender. He was kind and funny and clever. He was honest. He was good.

Too good to even begin to understand the kinds of horrifying things Holly was starting to believe about herself.

Holly stiffened in Jason's arms. Mumbling something incoherent, she stumbled to her feet and retreated toward the front door.

She didn't look back, not once. Not even before she went into the house.

Inside, she leaned back against the wall and listened to the drumming of her heart.

How could she be so cruel to Jason?

She asked herself the question at the same time she knew the answer.

She had to be mean to Jason. She had to get rid of him. She couldn't let him know what she really was.

Holly hauled in an unsteady breath. Lifting one edge of the draperies, she peeked out onto the front porch.

Jason hadn't moved from where she'd left him. He was still sitting on the railing, staring at the front door. His cheeks had spots of deep pink in them. His eyes looked as dead and empty as a TV set that wasn't turned on.

With a shake of his shoulders, Jason got up from the railing. He poked his hands in his pockets and shuffled down the stairs, his head bent.

Hoping to erase the image from her mind, Holly dropped the edge of the curtains and ran up to her room. She slammed the door, locked it, and flopped onto her bed.

She wanted to tell Jason. She wanted to tell Jason everything.

But how could she now?

How could she possibly tell him that she thought she was the one who killed Mr. Tollifson?

12

She was almost to the door.

Holly raised herself up on her tiptoes to see over the heads of the people in line in front of her. There wasn't much she could see: the somber paintings that lined the walls, the multicolored splash of the flower arrangements set around the room. And the coffin.

Holly felt her stomach go sour. She forced her eyes from the shiny brass handles at the ends of the coffin up to its polished wood sides. Even though she tried, she couldn't make herself look any farther.

"It's closed."

Sometime while Holly wasn't paying attention, Alex had slipped into line next to her. Startled, she looked up at him. "What?"

"I said it's closed." Alex put his arm around her and nudged her forward when the line moved again. "You don't have to be afraid to look. The coffin is closed."

"Is it? I can't see from here." Holly settled herself back down on her feet and tried her best to act like she didn't care in the least. It wasn't easy. One of the things she'd worried about most these past few days was coming here to Paxton's Funeral Home and looking at Mr. Tollifson.

Holly shivered. In spite of all her good intentions, she couldn't erase the picture from her mind, the picture of Mr. Tollifson lying on the ground under the weight of the panther, his mouth open in terror, the blue vein at the base of his throat throbbing.

Throbbing.

Throbbing.

"I said, you didn't think they'd leave it open, did you?"

Alex's voice jarred Holly back to reality. "I hadn't thought about it really," she said quickly to disguise her uneasiness. "I—"

"From what I heard, they couldn't leave the casket open."

Holly made a face. She should have known better than to think Alex might be here alone. He stepped aside and Laila came around from behind him.

Laila looked fabulous in her very short black skirt and a black cashmere sweater. She gave Holly the kind of smile a snake might give its unsuspecting dinner, eyeing her with a look that made it pretty clear she didn't think much of Holly's sensible navy chinos and her best green sweater.

Laila shuddered just enough to make her sleek black hair tumble over one shoulder. "They couldn't leave the casket open. The way Tollifson's body was torn up, I think they figured anyone who saw it would freak out. Can you imagine all the blood?"

A couple of kids waiting in line in front of them turned around and told Laila to stop being so disgusting. Laila didn't pay any attention. She looked directly at Holly, her eyes shining with something very much like excitement.

"I mean, I suppose a person would bleed an awful lot from their throat, wouldn't they?" Laila ran her fingers along her own throat from her chin to the hollow that showed just above the neckline of her sweater. Absently, she rubbed her index finger over the tiny blue vein that pulsed below the surface of her creamy skin.

Holly stared, mesmerized.

The overhead track lighting was dimmed to give Paxton's a peaceful atmosphere. The way the light hit Laila reminded Holly of the way Mr. Tollifson's face was lit in her dream: flushed and glowing with the first rays of the rising sun. The soft light emphasized the hollow of Laila's throat and highlighted the little throbbing vein.

Just like the vein in Mr. Tollifson's throat. The one Holly sliced open with her teeth.

The thought caught Holly off guard. She wrapped her arms around herself.

Laila was still talking, and Holly forced herself to ignore her neck and look at her face.

" . . . not any blood now, of course," Laila was saying. "But there must have been an awful lot of it. Some of the kids snuck up to the Hollow that night. They said the ground was soaked with blood. Soaked!"

"Gross!" A girl in back of them pushed out of line and headed for the ladies' room, her hand over her mouth.

Laila didn't even look at her. She went right on talking. "You've been up to the Hollow, Holly. You know what it looks like. Just picture all the grass sticky and caked with blood. They said there was a trail of it from the middle of the Hollow all the way to the tree where Tollifson's body was found." Laila sucked in a small breath and her eyes widened.

"Just imagine. His throat all ripped open and his body . . ." Laila jiggled her slender shoulders. "I hear every one of his bones was broken when he was dragged up in that tree."

"That's probably true." Alex stepped between Holly and his sister. "But maybe we should talk about something else, huh?"

"Thanks, but I don't need rescuing." In one brisk movement, Holly brushed Alex aside and stepped around him. She wished more than anything that Laila would talk about something else. But she wasn't about to let Laila know that. She raised her chin. "If you're waiting to see me turn green, Laila, you're going to have to wait a long time," she said. "You want to talk about what happened to Mr. Tollifson? Go right ahead. All the gory facts. All the bloody details. I'm not like these other wimps." Holly tossed a look at the kids around them. "It doesn't bother me in the least."

For a second, she thought Laila would take her up on her challenge. Her green eyes flashed at Holly.

She must have thought better of it. Or maybe Laila just decided she was bored. She looked over her shoulder, saw Tom and Amber waiting near the door and, without another word, turned away and went to stand with them.

As soon as she was gone, Alex put his arm around Holly again. He let it drift down from Holly's shoulder, resting it along the smooth curve where her hips met her waist. "She was out of line," he said, his eyes following Laila. "She shouldn't be so cruel. I guess she just can't help it. She has this ghoulish fascination with violent deaths."

"Is that why you're here?" Holly asked. "Because Laila is some sort of weirdo?" Holly didn't mean to make the question sound quite as vicious as it came out.

Alex didn't seem to mind. He laughed. "Me? I'm here to pay my respects. Pure and simple." He turned so that he was looking directly into Holly's eyes. "And why are you here?" he asked.

Why was she here?

The question had been tormenting Holly from the moment she decided to attend Mr. Tollifson's wake. But she couldn't let Alex know that. She couldn't let him know she was here for one reason and one alone: to find out the truth.

She wasn't sure how she'd do it, but she had to find out all she could about Mr. Tollifson's death. She wanted to know what really happened. She wanted to find out if she was involved.

Holly brushed off Alex's question. "I'm here for the same reason you're here," she told him as casually as she could. The line moved forward again before she could say anything else. Holly was glad for the interruption. It gave her a moment to compose herself.

That wasn't easy. In spite of the false front she'd

put up to impress Laila, Holly still felt queasy every time she thought about Mr. Tollifson. She swallowed her squeamishness and told herself now was as good a time as any to get started on finding the truth.

"Was it torn up?" She turned to Alex. "I mean, Tollifson's throat. Was it torn up? Or is that just the rumor going around school because it makes for a better story? I didn't see anything about it in the newspapers. *The Sun* said he'd been found dead in the Hollow. That's all. And *The Journal*, all it said was that Tollifson died of unknown causes. All this stuff about a wild animal, it might just be a story. You know, like the Los Gatos Panther."

"Yeah, a story." There was an expression almost like a smile on Alex's face. "My theory? I think Tollifson's coffin would be open if there was anything left of him to see."

In spite of the promise she'd made herself earlier to stay calm, Holly felt her stomach lurch. "Do the police have any idea why anyone would want to kill Tollifson?" she asked.

"Wrong place at the wrong time." Alex dismissed the question with a lift of his eyebrows. "That's what I think. And I don't think it's a question of *anyone* trying to kill him. I think it's more like *anything*."

"Then you believe in the panther?"

Alex pursed his lips. "I believe there are lots of things in this world that people will never under-stand," he said, his eyes glinting with a spark of green fire that made him look old and wise beyond his years. "Powerful, mysterious things. I think one of them is up at Panther Hollow. I also believe there are people around who know more about what happened to Tollifson than they're willing to say."

Was it Holly's imagination or did Alex look at her as if he knew she was hiding a secret?

Holly shook the thought away and tried to change the subject as quickly as she could. "But if there's someone in town who knows the truth, then we're talking *people*. People. Not panthers."

"Maybe." Again, Alex gave her one of those maddening half-smiles that made her wonder what was going on behind that gorgeous face of his. "Maybe there's more to this whole panther thing than anyone's willing to admit."

"Maybe," Holly agreed. Alex's responses to her questions didn't help much. She was no nearer finding the truth now than she was when she came to the funeral home.

There must be someone here who could tell her something.

Holly looked around the crowd. Mr. Lindblatten, the chemistry teacher, was standing by himself in the farthest corner of the funeral home. He was a good friend of Mr. Tollifson's, at least Holly thought he was. She'd seen them eat lunch together in the cafeteria.

They were about to move into the main room where the coffin was displayed when Holly excused herself. It didn't take her long to make her way over to Mr. Lindblatten.

• • •

"That was a little obvious, wasn't it?" Laila was loung-ing near the door that led to the downstairs room where coffee was being served. Alex leaned against the door frame and pinned his sister with a look. "We agreed we'd take this nice and slow and not arouse any suspicions."

"Nice and slow." Laila spat the words back at Alex. "You've been taking this nice and slow since the first day of school. I'm tired of waiting. I'm tired of putting up with that . . . that . . ." She looked over to where Holly was standing with Mr. Lindblatten and her top lip curled just enough to reveal her even, white teeth. "That *human*." She finished the sentence with a twist of her voice that made it clear it was not a compliment.

"You want to take your time and get to know her better." The corner of Laila's mouth curved into a sneer. "Well, we all know what you have in mind. Forget it, Big Brother. It's too dangerous. Let's find out once and for all. Tonight. Before she can do us any more harm."

"And what harm has she done us?" Alex propelled himself away from the wall. He balled his hands into fists and held them tight against his sides. "I asked you a question, Laila. I asked you what harm Holly has done any of us."

"You're a fool!" With an infuriating toss of her head that made Alex want to reach out and slap her, Laila turned and sauntered down the steps. There was no one down there, and she planted herself in the middle of the brown-and-white checked linoleum floor, her hands on her hips, and waited for her brother.

He didn't disappoint her.

Alex was down the steps in an instant. He ignored Tom and Amber who trailed behind him. He ignored Raymond and Lindsey who'd just come into Paxton's front door, sensed trouble, and followed.

He ignored them all and, pulling himself to a stop an arm's-length from Laila, he glared into her eyes. He didn't speak out loud. He didn't need to. He used the Gift and Laila heard him clearly, his voice as angry and intense as if he shouted the words.

"Tell me what harm she's done to us, Laila," Alex demanded. *"Tell me why you're so determined to hurt Holly. Or are you just jealous?"*

"Jealous!" Laila obviously hadn't even practiced using the Gift in ages. Her words were loud and clear inside Alex's head, but they sounded hollow, like a tape played without the bass being turned on. She was skilled enough to communicate her thoughts, but not her emotions. *"I'm not jealous,"* Laila said. Though her words were flat, her eyes blazed with anger. *"None of us are. But we're not stupid, either. If you keep summoning Holly every night, someone's going to find out. She's going to find out. And when she does, it will hurt us, Alex. She's going to hurt you. She's—"*

"She's my business, not yours." Alex turned away. Restless, he stalked across the room, turned, and came

back to his sister. "*We don't even know it's her, do we? We can't be sure. We don't know if it's Holly or someone else.*"

"*Who else could it be?*" Laila snorted her disagreement. "*None of this started until she came here. Everything was good. No one suspected—*"

"*No one suspects now,*" Alex snarled. "*And if you'd learn to control yourself and keep your head, we wouldn't need to worry. But no, not you. Not Laila. You think you can do anything you like and get away with it.*"

"*And you think you can—*"

"Wait a minute, you two."

It was Tom who spoke.

He didn't bother to use the Gift or maybe he was just too lazy to try. Alex felt a surge of disgust tighten around his stomach. He kept a stiff hold on his emotions while Tom elbowed between him and Laila.

Tom's eyes were nervous and frightened. There was a thin band of sweat just below his hairline.

His obvious fear was the only reason Alex forgave him for daring to butt in. At least he hasn't forgotten respect, Alex thought. At least Tom still knew who was Master and still had brains enough to be afraid.

"It isn't going to do us any good to fight," Tom said. He screwed up his face as if he expected a counterattack from Alex and he wasn't sure what form it would take. When Alex didn't move, Tom relaxed a little, but he still looked like a mouse caught between a trap and a hungry cat.

"Alex is right," Tom said, licking his lips and darting

a glance from Alex to Laila. "We don't know if Holly is the source of the Power we all feel. But if she is . . ." He drew in a deep breath. "If she is, it could put us all in danger. We can't ignore it, Alex, even though I know you'd like to wait. We all know you'd like to—"

"To what?" Alex pulled himself up to his full height. Tom was taller than him by an inch or two, but he knew that didn't matter a bit right now. He glared into Tom's eyes. He saw his own reflection in Tom's ballooning pupils, fiery red eyes and an expression clouded with a shadow that transformed his face.

Before any of them could move, Alex twisted one hand around Tom's collar. He raised the lanky boy a full five inches above the floor.

"Tell me. What do I want to do?" Alex asked, his voice silky with the threat of danger. He cast a look at Amber and Lindsey, Laila and Raymond. They were staring at him, their mouths open, fear written on their faces. "Since when do you—any of you—know my private thoughts?" With a gesture as careless as if he was whisking away a nagging insect, he dropped Tom to his feet and brushed him aside. He rounded on the group, staring down each of them in turn.

Only Laila held her ground. With a visible effort, she kept her chin steady.

"*We don't need to read your mind to know what you're thinking,*" she said, again using the Gift. "*All we have to do is watch you for a day or two. You're not acting like you have with the other human girls. It's always been different. Always. It's never been anything but a game to you. You've summoned girls before. Don't pretend you haven't. But none of them remembered the next day, did they? You heard Holly up there.*" Laila poked her chin toward the stairway.

"*You heard the kinds of questions she's asking. There's no reason for her to be this interested in Tollifson's death. Not unless she remembers. I think she does. I think she remembers too much. We've got to find out why, Alex. We've got to find out what she knows.*"

Alex didn't reply. He spun on his heels and went to stand at the yellow Formica table where a coffeepot bubbled next to a plate of fossilized brownies.

He hated it when Laila was right.

Alex drummed his fingers against the pitted table surface and admitted the hard facts to himself. They really had to do something about Holly. He wondered, though, had any of them taken the time to think there might be a reason Holly remembered so much?

Before he went any further, Alex instinctively shielded his thoughts, just in case any of the others would dare to use the Gift to probe his mind. Expertly, he reached out to theirs instead. He searched their thoughts, touching their shields lightly until he was sure it was safe to go on without being detected. Only Laila presented any sort of problem. That didn't stop Alex. Using powers Laila could not even imagine, he easily probed around her mind shields.

It didn't take long.

In a matter of seconds Alex was sure. None of them had thought of it. Not even Laila had realized that Holly might be the One.

A jolt like electricity barrelled its way up Alex's back and along his arms. It warmed his insides, as exciting as a drink of hot, fresh blood.

He hadn't even thought of it himself. Not until the other night when Holly beat him at the race.

But if she was the One . . .

Alex smiled.

If Holly was the One, things would be different. Very different.

Laila would be unhappy.

Alex's smile turned into a chuckle.

Laila would be very unhappy.

That in itself was enough to make him want to find out.

"You're right," Alex said out loud. He would not befoul the Gift by using it to surrender to Laila. He brushed his thumbs over the tips of his fingers and drew back into himself. If anyone came down the stairs now, he knew they would see nothing out of the ordinary, nothing more than a group of teenagers talking quietly.

"I would like to wait longer." Alex shoved his hands into the pockets of his leather jacket and, spinning around, he leaned against the table. "But maybe this is as good a time as any."

Pushing away from the table, he started up the steps. "Yes," he said before any of them could question him further. "I hate to admit it, but I think you're right. We do need to find out what Holly knows. We'll do it. And we'll do it tonight."

• • •

Mr. Lindblatten, the chemistry teacher, looked at Holly over the rims of his wire glasses. "Callison? Callison? Are you one of my students?"

"No, Mr. Lindblatten." Holly tried to erase any trace of anxiety from her voice. "I was one of Mr. Tollifson's biology students. I won't be taking chemistry until next year."

"Oh." Mr. Lindblatten turned away, dismissing her without another thought.

Holly wasn't about to give up so easily. She edged over to stand in front of Mr. Lindblatten. "I was just wondering," she said. "About Mr. Tollifson? I mean, he had some photographs, pictures he took up at Panther Hollow. I was wondering, Mr. Lindblatten, if you'd seen them?"

"Pictures?" Mr. Lindblatten blew into a large white hanky. He swiped the fabric under his nose a few times. "I saw them," he said. "Not very interesting. Raccoon. Cute, if you like that sort of pesty animal. Nothing to get excited about."

Holly bit at her lower lip. She might as well get it over with, she told herself. She gathered her courage and blurted out the words before she could convince herself to stop. "But Mr. Tollifson was excited," she said.

Her statement caught Mr. Lindblatten off guard. He blinked at her, his eyes like big brown balls behind his circular glasses. "You know, now that you mention it, Burt was pretty flustered that morning." Mr. Lindblatten spoke below his breath, his gaze fastened to the shiny casket in the next room. "Couldn't understand it myself. He said he'd just developed the pictures and weren't they really something. But then he showed them to me and I saw that they weren't all that great and . . ." Mr. Lindblatten gestured like a baseball umpire signalling that a runner was safe. "I didn't give it another moment's thought."

So far so good.

Holly tried again, thinking of the photograph hidden at the bottom of her dresser drawer, the picture of the panther pawprint. "Do you think there might have been other pictures?" she asked. "Pictures Mr. Tollifson didn't show you?"

"Other pictures?" Mr. Lindblatten scratched one hand through his gray hair. "I don't see why he wouldn't have—" He snapped his eyes to Holly's. "Are you saying this might have something to do with—?" Mr. Lindblatten looked from Holly to the casket.

"Ridiculous!" He rejected her suggestion outright. "Burt wasn't killed because of photographs. He wasn't killed because of anything. It was an accident. That's all. A terrible, sad accident." The more Mr. Lindblatten thought about it, the more certain he became. His voice rose with anger. "You'd be better off devoting your time and efforts to other things, young lady. What did you say your name was?"

Holly didn't wait around long enough for him to remember. Before Mr. Lindblatten could say another word, she retreated to the far end of the funeral home.

There was a small nook near the back door, a room only big enough for one chair and a telephone. Holly picked up the phone, dialed the weather, and pretended to be talking to someone while she looked around the crowd. Mr. Lindblatten was no help at all and she needed to find someone else she could question.

Was there anyone else who knew what Mr. Tollifson had found on Harper's Mountain?

"What, no Jason?"

Holly jolted out of her thoughts to find Ben Wiley staring down at her. She hung up the phone and watched Ben peer around as if he expected to see Jason come leaping to Holly's side at any second.

"Jason's working tonight." Holly knew that was true. Jason worked almost every Thursday night. What she didn't bother adding was that she hadn't talked to Jason lately. Not since last Sunday when she'd sent him away without even a good-bye.

"And Tisha?" Ben still didn't seem satisfied. He adjusted his glasses on the bridge of his nose and waited for Holly's answer.

"Tisha's helping her grandmother at the store tonight." Holly knew that was true, too. Tisha had begged her to wait to come to the funeral home tomorrow and Holly had promised she would. Tisha didn't have to know she was here tonight, too.

"I was hoping they'd be here," Ben said. "There's a new movie playing at the Grand and I thought we might all get together Saturday and—"

"Ben?" Holly launched into her questions before

Ben could get too far into his plans for the weekend. "Ben, does the newspaper office have a darkroom?"

"Sure." Ben pulled on his earlobe. "You have some pictures you want to—"

"Did Tollifson use it last week? A few days before he was killed?"

"Yeah!" Ben's eyes lit. "He did. Real early in the morning. He developed those goofy raccoon pictures— the ones he brought to biology class."

Holly squeezed her eyes shut. There was only one more thing she had to ask Ben and she prayed he'd give her the answer she wanted.

She opened her eyes and gripped Ben's sleeve with both hands. "Is there any way," she asked, "that some-one else could have seen those pictures before he ever got to biology?"

Ben wrinkled up his nose. "I suppose so." He shook his head. "Hey, what are you getting at? Do you think there was something in those pictures? Something someone would have killed Tollifson for?"

"I don't know." Holly answered honestly. "I really don't know. But if someone wanted to keep him quiet . . ."

She let the significance of her words trail into the silence. What she really wanted to say was the one thing she couldn't: That she hoped she would find some perfectly logical reason Mr. Tollifson had been killed. Someone trying to hide something. Someone trying to fool them all into believing there was some-thing deadly and frightening up at Panther Hollow.

Someone other than herself.

"It's an interesting theory." Ben's voice took on the kind of academic tone she'd heard him use in English literature class when he was trying to explain something no one else understood, not even the teacher. "Really interesting. You think Tollifson knew something and someone wanted to shut him up. I'll tell you what." Ben grabbed Holly's arm and tugged her toward the main room. "My dad's here. He's the Los Gatos cop assigned to the Tollifson case. I think this might be worth talking to him about."

"Your dad? A cop?" Holly knew the squeaky sound she heard was her own voice. She planted her feet, refusing to move another inch.

A cop.

Holly's hands trembled. Her insides got queasy.

That was all she needed. A cop. Someone who might realize there was more to her questions than simple curiosity. Someone who might suspect.

"I'll meet you in there." Holly pulled away from Ben and gave a meaningful look to the ladies' room door.

"Good." Ben rubbed his hands together and started toward the main room. "Dad's not buying all this stuff about a supernatural panther. He's been looking for a rational explanation to this whole thing. He's going to love this."

Holly didn't wait a moment longer. Before he could change his mind and decide to be a gentleman and wait for her, she turned around and headed out the back door.

She forced herself to walk slowly through Paxton's

parking lot. There was no use calling attention to herself. But once she was out on the street, she started to run. There was a bus coming down Main Street and Holly hurried toward it. It wouldn't take her anywhere near home, but she really didn't care. She needed to get away from here. Fast.

Holly jogged past the local convenience store and cut through the park. The bus was already stopped in front of the Grand Theater and she knew it would wait there a couple minutes. If she hurried . . .

It was the last thing Holly had a chance to think about.

The next thing she knew, a sharp blow landed on the back of her head.

She jerked to a stop. Through a daze, she felt her knees buckle. She saw the sidewalk come up. She felt her nose scrape against the cement.

She didn't have a chance to wonder what was happening before everything went black.

───13───

"You don't really think she can hurt us, do you?"

The voice made its way past the pain in Holly's head and coaxed her back to consciousness. It swirled through her mind like a half-heard sound carried by the wind—here one second, gone the next—until she wasn't sure if she heard the words or just imagined them.

"You agreed back at Paxton's."

This was another voice, another sound she caught not with her ears, but with her mind.

Holly shook her head. She wondered if whatever knocked her on the skull back in the park hadn't jarred loose the last of her sanity and sent her finally sliding over the edge into madness.

She could swear no one was talking.

But she heard voices. Voices in her head.

She couldn't tell who they belonged to. She couldn't tell if they were male or female. She only knew there were two of them.

And they were very angry at each other.

Holly didn't need to listen to their words to know that. She could feel it in her bones, sense it in the atmosphere. The bitterness of the voices vibrated around her like an electrical field, energized and dangerous. It hummed in the air and made the short hairs on the back of Holly's neck stand on end.

Anxious, Holly waited to hear more. But there was no more. All she could hear was the steady thrum of a car engine.

Holly lay back and took stock of her situation.

There was only one place she could be, she realized. The trunk of a moving car. She was on her back. Her hands were tied in front of her. Her legs were bound at the ankles. She was blindfolded and wedged into a space far too small for her, her head up against the spare tire, her back scraping against thin carpet and the bare metal beneath.

"I know what I said back there."

As suddenly as they'd stopped, the voices started again inside Holly's head. For some reason, she knew this was the first voice again. An edge of hostility tipped every one of the words. *"But it seems stupid to take the chance, doesn't it? What if she wakes up?"*

A woman's laugh pierced the silence, a sound Holly heard with her ears, not with her mind. It was a fierce laugh, a cruel laugh, and it crawled up Holly's spine and sent a swell of terror into her brain.

"If she wakes up, we'll take care of her. We'll have to. And you'll have to let us. If you don't—"

"If I don't, we'll all be in danger." The anger drained from the other voice. It sounded full of regret.

"That's right." Another peel of laughter reverberated through the car. *"Wouldn't that be a shame? You'd have to let us kill her."*

The words rumbled through Holly like the after-shock of an earthquake. Her stomach lurched into her throat.

There was no doubt who they were talking about.

She had incredible mind shields.

Alex looked down at Holly. She was cradled in his arms.

Sometime during the ride here, he sensed that she was conscious. Still, when he lifted her from the trunk, she was out again. He probed her mind then and there, and what he was able to read showed nothing unusual. Nothing to explain how or why she remembered his summoning.

Maybe Laila was right after all.

The thought made Alex press his lips together in a hard line.

Maybe it would take all their combined powers to read Holly.

Alex settled Holly closer to his chest. He let his instincts lead him up Harper's Mountain, his feet automatically finding their way along the familiar paths while his gaze rested on Holly.

Her head was rolled to one side and her copper hair trailed over the blindfold that still covered her eyes. She was like a floppy rag doll, and she looked— Alex hauled in an unsteady breath—she looked good enough to eat.

The others had gone on ahead to prepare the Hollow and Alex took his time catching up. He watched the way the moonlight etched Holly's features with an unearthly glow and a stab of some unfamiliar emotion pricked his heart, something that made him want to protect Holly, to keep her from Laila.

For he knew what Laila wanted tonight.

She wanted to prove that Holly was trouble. She wanted to prove that Holly was a threat. She wanted to get rid of Holly.

And what did he want?

Alex felt a smile lighten his expression.

He wanted Holly to be the One.

He dared admit the truth to himself.

He wanted Holly to be the One they were waiting for. Wanted it with all his being and all his heart and all of what was left of his soul.

For a moment, he was tempted to find out here and now. He could take Holly into the woods. He could say the chant himself. He was powerful, far more powerful than Laila and the others imagined. He just might have the strength to conduct the ceremony alone.

And if he didn't?

If he didn't, Alex knew, he'd be exposing both himself and Holly to unspeakable horrors.

It was too risky.

Alex calmed his excitement with the thought.

He had waited this long. He could wait a little longer. He would wait until they began the shared trance. Then he would summon Bast.

Not even Laila could stop him then. She would have to use her powers to help him. They all would.

Whether they liked it or not.

A hot stream like fire spread through Alex's gut and coiled around his heart.

"I have waited for you all this time," he whispered, looking down at Holly. "I can wait a little longer. I can wait and know for certain, once and for all."

They were in Panther Hollow.

Holly didn't need to see to know it. She could feel it in the air. She could tell it from the smell. She could hear it in the sounds that whispered close against her ears, as if the rocks that made the mountain, and the trees that clothed it, and the ancient, secret things that lived here long before even the trees and rocks, were telling her.

She fought her way back to consciousness to find herself lying on the ground, her arms and legs still tied, the blindfold tight around her eyes.

There were people all around her. Holly knew that, too. They were standing in a circle, staring down at her. She could feel their eyes. She could sense their thoughts.

Holly didn't bother to stop and wonder how she could do it, she only knew it was true.

She could read their minds, loud and clear, like radio signals being sent directly into her brain, and what she read sent an icy claw of fear around her throat and made her heart pound against her ribs.

They felt contempt for her.

They felt disgust.

They felt she was nothing more than a pest, like

a tiny bug that irritates picnickers and gets squashed because of it.

Even if Holly wanted to follow where her train of thought was leading, she didn't have the time. Before she knew it, she heard the shuffle of feet and she knew that those gathered in the circle were moving closer together.

"Join hands." In Holly's head, she heard the same voice she'd heard back in the car, the one that seemed so cruel. Now there was no emotion in it. It was just a sound, flat and distant, like an echo in a cave.

"We'll go down together," the voice instructed. *"If there are no objections?"* The voice seemed to be expecting some opposition.

Holly waited, too, every fiber of her being tensed.

There was no protest.

"We'll meet outside her shields," the voice said. *"And start the probe together. We'll begin . . . Now!"*

Silence settled on the Hollow.

The wind died. The small animals that lived in the undergrowth stopped their scurrying. The owls that hunted from high up in the trees settled on their branches and watched.

All of them quiet.

All of them waiting.

Holding her breath, Holly waited, too.

The first experimental probe touched Holly's mind so abruptly, it forced the air out of her lungs with a *whoosh*. The touch was not physical. That wouldn't have been nearly as terrifying.

This contact was without form or substance, a sensation that stabbed her right behind the eyes. It was as if someone was poking around in there, trying to get inside her head.

Instinctively, Holly slapped aside the probe.

It only got worse.

The pinprick sensation came again. Sharper this time. Stronger than before.

Holly tried to cover her head. That was impossible, her hands were tied. She tried to turn away. That was useless. Her kidnappers were all around her.

Before she could stop them, they were inside her mind.

Holly felt each presence as it entered. There were six of them, and she knew exactly what they thought of her the moment they invaded her head.

Distrust. Dislike. Indifference. Resentment. Hate. A hate so strong it washed over Holly like a cold wave and left her trembling.

But nothing prepared her for the final presence. Nothing equipped her to deal with the awesome strength of it, the amazing power, the undeniable certainty that it was here not to read her thoughts like the others were, but to judge her.

She knew that judgment would seal her fate.

The probe strengthened and Holly whimpered. It went deeper, and she heard herself cry out.

And then it stopped.

Like a door slammed shut by a howling wind, the examination was cut off. Holly fell back against the damp grass, her breathing fast and shallow, her head spinning.

A man's voice filled her ears and reverberated through the Hollow.

"We call on the goddess Bast." He pronounced the words slowly, as if they had great power.

"No!" A woman shrieked. "You can't. You can't do this. Why do you want—?"

"You can't stop it now." Was it Holly's imagination, or was there a trace of amusement in the voice? It sounded very pleased with itself.

It also sounded familiar.

Holly tried to place the voice and got nowhere. Her head felt like it was stuffed with cotton balls. She fought against a billow of dizziness that made it hard to think.

"I have summoned Bast," she heard the man say. She wasn't sure how she knew it, but she was certain he was looking at the others, daring them to challenge him. "Are any of you powerful enough to send her away? Do any of you dare to deny her the honor of testing this person? Of learning if she is the One?"

"The One?" The woman choked on the words. "She can't be. It's impossible. I—" Her final words were cut off by the man's chilling laugh.

The sound shattered the night. It wheeled through the Hollow and spiraled into the sky. It faded among the stars, a sound lost to both earth and heaven.

Silence settled like a thick blanket that pressed against Holly's ears.

A minute went by. Then another, until Holly felt like she would scream.

But she couldn't. No matter how hard she tried. She felt as if all the air had been sucked out of the Hollow. There was nothing left. Nothing but a quiet as deep as the night, a silence as bottomless as the sea and as endless and meaningless as time itself.

Nothing could violate a silence this profound—Holly knew it in her bones—just as nothing could call back the summons the man had made, the call to the goddess Bast.

The name meant nothing to Holly, but it tickled something at the back of her mind. Something half-remembered. Something important.

"Bast." She felt her lips form the strange word, heard her own voice, low and foreign-sounding, as if it belonged to someone else.

"Bast."

No sooner had the name passed Holly's lips the second time than a roaring wind ripped through the Hollow. A clap of thunder smashed the night and a blinding light burst overhead, a light so bright Holly could see it even through her blindfold.

It wasn't lightning. It didn't flash and disappear. This light exploded into flames that crackled somewhere above Holly's head. It blazed against her cheeks and made her whole body feel like it was on fire.

"Bast, embodiment of Re."

The firestorm seemed to be the man's sign to continue. He wasn't speaking anymore. He was chanting, the words a singsong pattern that rose and fell in tempo with the rhythm of the blood in Holly's veins.

"Bast, goddess of the cat. Giver and bestower. Creator of our Power. We offer you bread. We hold out milk to you. We honor you with the gifts of the Nile. We ask you to hear us and to answer our call."

His words faded, replaced by a strange noise. At first, it came only from the man. Then the others joined in, each voice taking up the chorus. They weren't saying words. They were making sounds. Animal sounds.

The sensations came in a jumble after that. The heat of the fire. The dazzling light. The noises that wound through Holly's mind and confused her senses and turned her thinking upside down and around again.

Still, the voices continued on and on. Sometimes Holly almost thought she could understand them. Other times, their words and sounds dissolved into growls.

The combination of sensations destroyed all sense of time and place. It sent Holly spinning out of control and demolished all of what was left of Holly Callison. It left her empty. Open. Ready.

Ready for the change.

It started slowly.

A tingle like electricity ripped up Holly's back. She winced and jiggled her shoulders, trying to make the feeling go away.

It didn't.

It only got stronger.

The tingle became a jolt, the jolt spread from Holly's back into her arms and legs.

She heard herself scream. But by that time it was too late.

Holly stretched her legs and the ropes binding her ankles snapped. She crouched on her hands and knees and the cords around her wrists fell to the ground.

The tips of her fingers tingled as each fingernail grew into a claw. Her back prickled where sleek black fur grew. Her teeth throbbed and her jaw ached and her eyeteeth grew long and sharp and powerful enough to rip the throat from any prey.

No!

The protest ricocheted through Holly's mind. This couldn't be happening. It was a hallucination. It was a joke. It was a cruel trick of some kind, a not-so-funny prank that called on the horrors of her worst nightmares.

No!

She tried to scream but the only sound that came from Holly was her new voice, one that roared its hunger for blood.

The sound must have staggered those around her. As abruptly as their chanting started, it stopped, cut short by gasps of surprise. As soon as the chanting stopped, so did the transformation.

Holly fell back on the grass. She felt the fire above her fade at the same time her claws retracted. The fur on her body and legs disappeared. Her teeth shrunk. Sobbing, she rolled over on her back and yanked the blindfold away from her eyes.

Amber, Lindsey, Tom, and Raymond were standing in a loose circle around her. They were gaping at her, their mouths open, their eyes scrunched up in disbelief.

Holly was too dazed to even begin trying to figure out what they were doing here. She groaned and turned her head.

In the last flickers of the dying fire she saw Laila standing away from the others, close to where the woods met the edge of the Hollow. Laila's body was rigid. Her eyes were dark with resentment and horror and another emotion Holly could only interpret as awe.

But she wasn't looking at Holly.

She was staring directly across the Hollow.

Holly didn't have to follow Laila's gaze to know who she was looking at. Though every muscle in her body protested the sudden movement, Holly turned over.

Alex was standing directly above her. He was smiling. Smiling like a kid on Christmas morning.

Dropping down on one knee, Alex bent and kissed Holly's cheek. Alex's eyes were warm. Taking both her hands in his, he helped Holly to her feet and drew her into the circle of his arms.

"Welcome," he said, his voice a whisper against her hair. "We've been waiting for you for a very long time."

———14———

"No!"

Holly's heart was racing. Her breaths were shallow. Jerking back, she batted away Alex's hands and stared at him.

Alex's face glowed. There was a glimmer of affection in his eyes, a tender expression that transformed his face and made him more handsome than ever.

"You don't understand." Alex smiled and, opening his arms, invited Holly into the shelter of his embrace. "You don't know what—"

"No!" With every last ounce of energy she had left, Holly swung out at him. She felt her palm smack against Alex's cheek, had the quick impression of his angelic expression crumpling with surprise, his shoulders pulling back, his hands curling into fists.

She didn't wait to see any more.

Swiveling around, Holly pushed past Amber and Lindsey and headed toward the woods.

She didn't stop to think where she was going.

She didn't care.

She only knew she had to get as far away from here as she could. As far away from Them.

Holly dared a quick look over her shoulder.

Alex had disappeared, but Amber, Lindsey, Tom, and Raymond were still there. They were all talking at once, waving toward the woods, urging Laila to do something.

And Laila?

Laila was standing exactly where Holly saw her last. Anyone passing by might have mistaken her for a statue, she was so still. Except for her eyes. Laila's eyes flared. And they watched Holly's every move.

Holly turned away and stumbled into the woods. Her knees felt like jelly. Her heart was pounding so hard, she couldn't catch her breath.

She forced herself to go on, pushing her way through the low-hanging branches that whipped her cheeks, stumbling and falling and struggling to her feet only to trip again a few yards farther down the path.

Holly groaned and pulled herself up on her knees. She wiped away the tears and blood that ran down her cheeks, forced herself to stand and, half-running, half-crawling, headed deeper into the woods on Harper's Mountain.

Up ahead, she could see the outline of the old camp building, the one she'd searched the night of the homecoming bonfire.

Could she hide inside? she wondered. Could she keep out of sight until the others were gone?

Holly was almost to the rickety steps when she heard a soft noise behind her. Like something dropping out of a tree.

She stopped and glanced over her shoulder.

There was nothing there.

But the hairs on the back of her neck weren't prickling for nothing. Holly knew that. Every muscle tensed and ready to run, she looked from side to side.

There was nothing out there, either, nothing but the trees that surrounded the little clearing like sentinels, silent and unmoving.

Taking a cautious step forward, Holly peered ahead.

That's when she saw it. A deeper shadow that filled the darkness between her and the steps, a blurry shape like a puff of smoke that rolled close to the ground and was gone, even before she was sure she'd seen it.

Holly swiped one trembling hand across her eyes.

"It's nothing." Holly didn't sound any more assured than she felt, but she kept talking out loud, trying to give herself the courage to continue. "Just your imagination. Like the stuff that happened in the Hollow. It's—"

Someone grabbed Holly from behind. Her words turned into a scream. A split second later her shriek was smothered by a hand that clamped over her mouth. She was spun around and around again, until her head got dizzy and her legs turned wobbly and her screams tapered into one long moan of fear and helplessness.

Holly went limp. If it wasn't for the strength of the arms around her, she would have fallen. Her assailant propped her against the camp building and pinned her there, her nose pressed into the front of his leather jacket.

How long they stood like that, Holly didn't know.

She only knew how scared she was. And how miserable. And how each time she sobbed, it made her chest ache and her throat hurt and her head pound.

After what felt like a very long time, her crying eased up. When it did, so did the pressure of the hand over her mouth.

"Promise you won't scream." It was Alex's voice. Alex who held her, his chest rock hard against hers. He moved back a fraction of an inch, far enough to be able to look down at Holly.

Even in the dark, she could read the look in his eyes. It urged her to surrender. It also made it very clear that if she didn't, he wouldn't hesitate to do whatever was necessary to keep her quiet.

"Promise?" This time it was more than just a request. Alex's question reached Holly's ears at the same time another, unspoken message made its way into her brain.

"Stop fighting me."

The command came loud and clear.

Before Holly could even realize what was happening, all the defiance drained out of her. She slumped back against the building.

Alex greeted her obedience with a broad smile. Slowly, just to make sure she wasn't trying to trick him, he moved his hand away. Satisfied she wouldn't start screaming again, he let go of a breath and settled his hand on Holly's shoulder. But he didn't move. He was still close, so close, Holly could feel his heart beating frantically against hers.

"You're afraid. I know you are." Alex's voice didn't betray his excitement the way his heartbeat did. It was calm, almost gentle. "Believe me, I know. I was afraid the first time, too."

The words hit Holly like a slap and sent a fresh wave of hysteria blasting through her. Jerking to attention, she looked over Alex's shoulder, back toward the Hollow. "No! It can't be true that it ever happened to you," she said, her voice rising with each word. "It didn't happen to me. Not for real. It was some kind of trick. You gave me some kind of drug. I—"

"Holly, Holly, Holly." There was just enough amusement in Alex's voice to dampen the fire of Holly's words. He cupped her chin in one hand and raised her face to his. "It's not something to be afraid of," he said. "You'll see. It's a Gift. A wonderful Gift. Don't you see how lucky you are? Don't you see what it means?"

"I can't. I can't think. My brain is all confused and my head feels like it's going to explode." Holly rubbed her hands over her face. If she stayed this close to Alex for one second longer, she was sure she would shatter into a million little pieces. Elbowing past him, Holly moved a few feet away and dragged in a long breath of cool night air. She ran her fingers through her hair.

It was just hair.

She chafed her hands up and down her arms. Just hands.

Just arms.

She looked down at her body and her legs and her

feet, and turned to Alex, a question in her eyes.

"I don't understand," Holly said, her words trembling on the edge of a sob. "I want to understand, Alex. I do. But it doesn't make any sense. How can I be—?" She couldn't say the words. "It isn't possible," she said, and hot tears rolled down her cheeks. "It can't be real. It's like that awful dream I've been having ever since we came to Los Gatos."

"Ah, the dream."

Something about the way Alex said the words sent a shiver up Holly's spine. It wasn't pleasure she heard in his voice. Not exactly. It was more like satisfaction. The kind of satisfaction a cat might have after swallowing a canary.

Alex grinned at her. "You haven't had a chance to piece it all together yet, have you?" he asked. "I don't blame you. Everything's happening so fast. But don't you see? It wasn't a dream."

"Wasn't a—?" The words whirred through Holly's brain like a buzz saw, chopping apart every last shred of everything she thought was real. "You can't be serious. It can't be true. I—"

"You look good enough to eat!" Alex stepped forward and took Holly's hands in his.

"No." Holly shook her head. She tried to pull away but Alex wouldn't let her. He held on tight and smiled at her and his teeth glinted in the moonlight.

"You're trying to fool me," Holly said, desperately struggling to make sense of everything that was happening. "You're trying to confuse me. But you can't.

I remember I told you at the homecoming dance. I told you I had a dream. I repeated those words, 'You look good enough to eat.' Don't try to make this any worse, Alex. Don't try to make me think you know things you can't possibly know."

Alex lifted his shoulders in an elegant little gesture that made his leather jacket crinkle. "I'm not trying to fool you. I can prove it. I'll admit, you did tell me about the dream at homecoming. But you didn't tell me all of it, did you? Okay, then explain something else to me. Tell me how I know you dream about the panther?"

Whatever hopes Holly had that there was some logical explanation for all this were dashed with those words.

Alex knew it, and he hurried on. "You didn't tell me about that, did you? You didn't tell anyone. You didn't tell Tisha, 'cause she's already too scared. You didn't even tell Jason. Good old Jason! I wonder what he would say if he knew the girl he loved had a . . . a . . ." Trying to find the right words, Alex tapped his index finger against his top lip.

"A darker side." He settled on that and smiled. "Would it matter to him, you think? It matters to me, but not in the same way. You see, I know all about your dreams, Holly. I'm the one who summoned you into them. I'm the one who watched you walk through the school halls. The one you met in the newspaper office. The one who said, 'You look good enough to eat.' " Alex moved a step closer and put his hand under Holly's chin. With his thumb, he traced the outline of her mouth.

"Do you remember what happened after that?" he asked, his words a whisper against her lips. "After that, I almost kissed you. I wanted to. I would have done it, too, if it wasn't for Laila." Alex's expression darkened. He tossed a look toward the Hollow and his mouth twisted into a sneer. "She used her power to send you back. To wake you up."

Holly closed her eyes, blocking out all the wild emotion in Alex's expression. She was tired. Very tired. She wished she could forget everything that happened tonight, everything that had happened since her family came to Los Gatos. She wished she could just sink into Alex's arms and get lost in his touch.

But she couldn't. Not when there was still so much troubling her. The first thing was almost too horrifying to put into words. Holly forced herself to raise her eyes to Alex.

"My parents," she asked "are they—?"

"No." Alex chuckled. "It isn't something that's inherited. It's a Gift. Like I told you. None of our parents know and you can't tell yours." He wouldn't speak again until she nodded her agreement.

When she did, Alex pulled Holly into his arms. He propped his chin on top of her head and hugged her hard against him and the words fell out of him in a tumble. "There's so much for you to learn!" he said. "So much I want you to know. I didn't dare believe any of this could happen. But after that race the other night, the one where you beat me, I started to think maybe. Just maybe. I was so happy back there in the Hollow. So happy to know you're the One! Oh Holly, it's too good to be true!"

"The One?" Like a sleepwalker, Holly repeated the words mechanically. She pulled back and gave Alex a questioning look. "The One what?"

This time, Alex laughed out loud. "The One we've been waiting for. There are six of us, you see. Me, Laila, Tom, Raymond, Amber and Lindsey. And it's no accident we've all been brought to this place in this time. It's more than just coincidence that we've all ended up in a town called Los Gatos, a town that's already got a legend about panthers. There's something important we have to do here. But before we could get started, we needed the Power of Seven. Number seven. That's you."

It was all too much for Holly. Fighting to clear her mind, she kneaded her temples and shook her head. "But why?" She tried to stay calm, but it just didn't work. Her question rose up on a sob. "It's not something I want. I don't like changing like that. It scares me and it hurt."

Alex caressed her cheek. "I know. But now that we know what you are, I can teach you to channel your Gift. To change only when you want to change. It hurt back in the Hollow because you were fighting it. When you learn to flow with it, it's as easy as . . ."

He didn't bother to explain. He showed her.

One instant he was Alex. Tall, wonderful, gorgeous Alex.

The next second . . .

Holly sucked in a breath of surprise.

The next second there was a panther in front of her—the same sleek panther who haunted her dreams.

"You see how easy it is?" The words reached Holly's mind. She knew they were coming from him. The panther. Alex.

It didn't hurt, not even a little. As a matter of fact, it's an awesome feeling. The whole world is different once you change. You'll see, once you let yourself accept what you are, everything will be wonderful. And our power—" The panther's chest rose and fell with excitement. His eyes sparked.

"Together, our power will be incredible."

With unearthly quickness, the panther sprang. Holly fell back, the panther's front paws on her shoulders, its terrible teeth only inches from her throat.

This is what it was coming to.

The thought flashed through Holly's mind right before she slammed into the weathered siding of the camp building.

All these weeks, this is where her dream was leading her. Here. To this time, and this place, to the sight of the panther's razor-sharp teeth flashing in the moonlight and the feel of his claws piercing her skin.

Her dream had led her to one, electrifying realization: that she was like Alex, a kindred spirit trapped in a human body. A soul mate only he could free.

The thought made Holly's soul catch flame.

Her heart pounding in perfect rhythm to his, she ran her hands over Alex's face.

His fur was soft and as luxurious as velvet. His pulse raced in his neck.

For the briefest of moments, Holly's thoughts flashed back to all the things she'd thought she wanted out of life: a home, a family, a meaningful career, friends like Tisha who would stand by her through thick and thin, a great guy like Jason.

She nuzzled her face in the panther's muscular shoulders and was rewarded with a purr.

Holly smiled.

She'd been wrong. Very wrong.

This was all she needed from life, this feeling of wanting to be one with Alex, wanting it with her whole heart and her whole soul and her whole body. This was what it meant for her to be alive.

The awareness made Holly's heart pound furiously. Raising her head, she gazed into Alex's green eyes.

They didn't look like emeralds anymore. They weren't hard and cold as ice. They looked like green fire and they burned through the last of Holly's defenses and destroyed all that was left of the girl she used to be.

"Lift your head!"

The command rang through Holly's mind. She was powerless to resist.

Holly tipped back her head.

The panther opened its mouth. Wider. Until she could feel its breath, hot against her neck.

"More!"

Again the voice commanded her and again she had to obey.

Closing her eyes, she leaned back against the building. She felt the panther's jaws fasten around her throat.

The pain was fierce and sharp, but it lasted only for an instant. Just as quickly, the bite softened to a nuzzle, the nuzzle turned into a kiss. The soft fur beneath Holly's fingers changed to a leather jacket, and Alex was there in front of her.

His hands were on her shoulders, his lips were on her skin. He trailed a series of kisses down Holly's neck, his mouth hot, his teeth nipping at the delicate skin at the base of her throat.

Holly heard herself sigh at the same time Alex broke away.

"It isn't easy for us," he said, his eyes round and dark with longing. "We have a wonderful gift, but it demands great sacrifices. You'll understand some day. You'll learn to control your changing. You'll learn to let it happen only when you want it to. We're affected by strong emotions, Holly. All of us. If we're very worried, or happy. If we're excited . . ." He smiled and ran one finger down Holly's cheek.

"It can cause the change without warning. That's what was happening to you. In your dreams. You were scared about coming to a new school, weren't you? That's what started it. Then, every time we were together, I knew you were as nervous and keyed up as I was. I could handle it. I'm more skilled. I could keep myself from changing. But you couldn't. Once you fell asleep and all your barriers were down . . . Oh, Holly! Don't you see? That's why I could never show you how I really feel about you. I couldn't risk losing control. I couldn't risk changing in front of you. Now . . . now I don't have to worry."

Alex didn't explain anymore. He didn't have to. He kissed her and his kiss explained everything. All he thought and all he felt. All the sadness that had filled him such a short time ago, when he thought they could never be together. All the happiness that was inside him now that he knew Holly was the One.

Holly slid her arms around Alex's neck and linked her fingers behind his head. She made a little groan of protest when Alex moved away.

"No more for now." Alex ran his hands over Holly's hair and wrapped his arm around her shoulders. "Soon. But not now. When you're trained. When you're skilled. When you learn your heritage and your power. Then . . ." Alex's voice trembled with emotion. "Then you'll sit at my right hand and together, there's nothing we won't be able to do!"

It was the promise of a lifetime together and it was all Holly could ever hope for. Smiling a dreamy smile, she leaned her head on Alex's shoulder and let him lead her back to the Hollow.

They were almost there when a disturbing memory nudged the contentment from Holly's mind. She stiffened and jerked to a stop.

"Alex?" Holly hated to spoil the peaceful atmosphere that surrounded them like a fluffy blanket, but she knew she had no choice. "Alex," she asked, "what about Mr. Tollifson?"

Alex must have been as lost in dreams as she was. He blinked at her. "Huh?"

"I'm willing to accept all of this," Holly said. "I'm willing to accept both of us for what we are. But what about Mr. Tollifson? I could never live with myself if I knew I killed him."

A dark expression erased the look of delight from Alex's face. He turned his back on Holly. "Forget about Mr. Tollifson," he said, his voice odd and thick. "We'll talk about it some other time. Some time when you're not so tired and—"

"No!" The uncertainty felt like a stranglehold on Holly's throat. She couldn't stand it anymore. Gripping Alex's arm with both her hands, she spun him around to face her. "I have to know, Alex. And I have to know now. I can't forget that last dream I had. The look on Mr. Tollifson's face. I can't forget . . ." Holly's words dissolved into tears.

Alex's shoulders slumped. His eyes were infinitely sad. He looked like his heart had just been broken in two. "I didn't want you to know," he said. "In case it might make you change your mind. About me." Was it a trick of the moonlight, or were there tears glimmering in his eyes?

Instinctively, Holly reached out for Alex. She stroked his cheek. "Tell me," she whispered. "I have to know. And please, don't worry. Nothing could change the way I feel about you."

It was so long before Alex said anything, Holly thought he might not answer at all. He stared somewhere over her head, his eyes empty, as if the green fire that had burned in them such a short time ago had been smothered by some memory too painful to speak. Finally, a shudder trembled its way across his shoulders. His chest rose and fell.

"A panther blundered into that trap of Tollifson's," Alex said, his voice so quiet, Holly had to strain to hear it. "There really was nothing else I could do."

Holly felt her breath close around the painful ball of emotion that wedged in her throat. "You?"

Alex shook his head. "I had no choice," he said, almost to himself. "You see, if we're caught when we're panthers, we can't change back. Ever. Not until we're free again. Holly!" Her name rose from his lips like the cry of a wounded animal. Alex grabbed Holly's arms and held them in a grip as desperate as it was powerful.

"I couldn't let that happen. I had to do something. I was frantic. I wasn't thinking. I got rid of Tollifson and freed the panther from the trap. But it didn't wait around. Just darted off into the woods. That's when I realized it wasn't any of the others. Not the shape-shifters I knew. Holly, it was you."

"And you were forced to kill Mr. Tollifson because of me? Because I was careless enough to get caught?" Holly ignored her own tears. She stroked Alex's neck and rubbed his shoulders, whispering comfort in his ear. "I'm sorry," she said. "I didn't know. I . . . I promise. We'll never talk about it again."

Her words seemed enough to satisfy Alex. With the back of his hand, he swiped at his cheeks. "We have a lot to think about," he said, starting off back toward the Hollow. "We'll need to plan your initiation."

It was just like Alex to try and spare her feelings.

Holly found herself smiling and following his lead. "Initiation?" The word had a mysterious ring to it and she turned it over in her mouth like some weird food, checking out all its possibilities.

Alex saw the uncertain look on Holly's face. "It's not as bad as it sounds," he said, quickly trying to reassure her. "We won't even attempt it until we know you can change without any discomfort."

By this time they were back at the Hollow.

The others were there waiting. They eyed Alex nervously, like they weren't sure what he might do, and Holly couldn't help but notice that they looked at her with open resentment.

Alex didn't miss it, either.

Taking Holly's hand, he led her into the clearing. No more than two feet from where the others stood, he stopped and draped his arm protectively around Holly's shoulders.

He looked at each of them in turn, his gaze stopping and staying on Laila. "Holly is the One," Alex said, his voice echoing around the Hollow. "You saw it with your own eyes. She is one of us. Her coming gives us the Power of Seven. We must welcome her as part of our family."

For a long time, nobody moved. They looked down at the ground. They looked at each other. They looked at Alex.

That seemed to be enough to help them make up their minds.

Raymond was the first to come up. Dragging his feet, not daring to meet her eyes, he hugged Holly in an awkward embrace. "Welcome," he said.

The others followed, one by one.

Tom looked tense. Lindsey looked embarrassed. Amber looked distinctly envious.

And Laila?

Laila never moved.

Crossing her arms over her chest, Laila stared at her brother. They didn't say a word to each other. They didn't have to. Holly knew there was a mind conversation running between them.

But no matter how hard she tried, Holly couldn't pick up any of their words. Alex and Laila must have been deliberately shielding their thoughts.

Curious, Holly let her gaze dart back and forth between them. It didn't take long before she realized she didn't have to read minds to know what Alex and Laila were saying. She could read it on their faces. And what she saw there made her blood run cold and her heart stop.

Alex and Laila didn't just dislike each other.

Holly read it in every line of Alex's face, every sharp look Laila tossed his way.

This had nothing to do with sibling rivalry.

This was hatred, pure and simple, a hatred so old and deep-seated, Holly couldn't even begin to under-stand it.

Jiggling her shoulders, Holly tried to shake off the bad vibrations that radiated from Alex and Laila like the heat from a fire. The sounds of their silence filled

Holly's ears until it felt like her head would burst. It filled the Hollow from one end to the other.

After what seemed like an eternity, Laila flinched as if she'd been punched.

Holly let go of a long breath. She watched Laila's face go ashen, her eyes widen, her mouth open.

And she knew that Alex had won.

Even so, it took a couple more minutes for Laila to step forward. Every inch of her stiff with outrage, she looked Holly up and down. "Welcome," Laila said. She sounded like she was going to choke on the word.

Holly heard Alex chuckle and felt his hand at the small of her back, nudging her forward. "You must embrace and be friends," he said.

Holly looked at him doubtfully.

"Go ahead," Alex urged. "We're all part of one. All children of the goddess Bast. Laila is as much your sister now as she is mine."

Holly made a sour face. It was a look that didn't last long. By the time she turned to Laila, she was smiling, the kind of self-satisfied, superior little smile Laila always used on those she thought were beneath her. She gave Laila the briefest of hugs. "I hope we can be friends," Holly said.

Laila didn't answer. Spinning on her heels, she stomped out of the Hollow and was out of sight before any of them could stop her.

15

"We call on the goddess Bast, embodiment of Re, goddess of the cat. Giver and bestower. Creator of our Power."

Alex's voice rang over Harper's Mountain. It was answered by the voices of the others, repeating his words. Their chant filled the cold night air and rose up to the huge full moon that hung over Panther Hollow like an orange ball.

"We offer you bread."

"We offer you bread." Holly joined the others in repeating the words of the sacred chant. She knew she should be looking straight ahead, keeping her eyes on Alex who was standing at the center of the group. But she couldn't help herself, she had to dart a look around the circle.

They were all dressed alike, boys and girls, in long white robes that just skimmed the tops of their sandaled feet.

They looked beautiful. Holly had to admit it to herself.

They all looked beautiful. Mysterious. Special.

Even Laila, who hadn't spoken one more word to Holly since that night in the Hollow, even Laila looked great. Like the other girls, her hair was loose around her shoulders. It gleamed like a splash of glossy black paint against the white of her robe. Laila's cheeks were flushed with excitement, her eyes sparkled. She looked so good, it was almost possible to overlook the dark smudges under her eyes, telltale signs that revealed that Laila had spent many a sleepless night these past weeks.

Holly pushed the uncomfortable thought to the back of her mind and finished looking around the circle from Laila to Raymond, from Raymond to Amber, from Amber to Tom, from Tom to Lindsey. Like Holly, they were all wearing thin bands of golden metal around their foreheads. The metal glinted in the moonlight and made them look like kings and queens.

Only Alex's outfit was different. His robe was the same, so was the band around his head. But he was also wearing a spectacular collar of green, blue, and white beads that looked like it came right out of a museum.

"We hold out milk to you."

Alex's voice jarred Holly back to reality.

"We hold out milk to you." She repeated the chant along with the others.

"We honor you with the gifts of the Nile. We ask you to hear us and to answer our call."

No sooner had their voices faded into the night than a flame popped out of thin air and hung over the circle, directly above Alex's head. The fire was brighter than last time, a huge yellow flame that sparked and flashed.

Holly raised her face to the fire. She felt it blister against her cheeks. She felt it burn, even through her long white gown. She felt it heat the gold band around her forehead until it felt like the metal would brand her skin.

Still, she couldn't look away.

Bast's fire was beautiful.

As if in a dream, Holly felt Alex take hold of her hands. He led her into the center of the circle, placed his hands on her head and whispered a long series of mysterious words.

When he was done, he kissed Holly's forehead and looked into her eyes.

"I speak for Bast," he said, his voice low, his eyes ablaze with the reflection of the divine fire. "She asks if you are ready to accept the Gift."

Now that the moment had come, Holly found herself strangely nervous.

It was ridiculous, of course. They had practiced every moment of the ceremony these past few weeks. They had been over everything that would be said. Everything that would happen.

She was ready.

Holly looked into Alex's eyes.

She was ready to be with him forever.

"Yes," she said, repeating the words exactly as she'd been taught. "I receive Bast's Gift with joy. I discard my base human form. I become one with Bast, goddess of the cat."

The weeks of practice had paid off. This time the

change didn't take long at all. It went smoothly, quickly, painlessly, just like Alex had promised.

One second she was Holly, looking into Alex's eyes. The next second, she was a panther, and he was looking down at her, his face so filled with breathless wonder and desire that it made Holly's heart ache inside her.

Alex knelt before her, one hand on either side of her head.

"I speak for Bast," he said again, his voice ringing with authority. "And in the name of Bast, goddess of the cat, I welcome you with joy. I make you one with those who travel the night in her image. I name you kinswoman of Sekhmet, the lion goddess, I call you handmaiden of Amon-Re, king of the gods, I declare you a server of Seth who guides our actions and commands our Power. I call you sister and pledge my loyalty."

"Sister."

"Sister."

Each of the others came up and placed their hands on Holly's head. When they were done, they moved to stand in a circle around her, their hands joined. They swayed back and forth, harsh, guttural sounds coming from their mouths as they, too, changed into panthers.

One by one, they were beside Holly and even in their panther forms, she knew who they were. Tom and Raymond, Amber and Lindsey. Laila.

Holly ignored them all. She turned to Alex.

"Tomorrow there will be time enough for you to

learn more about our ways. Alex's voice came into her mind. He turned and, swift as lightning, raced into the night. *"Tonight,"* he called, *"tonight, we celebrate!"*

One by one, they followed him into the woods on Harper's Mountain, their passing no more than a ripple in the shadows.

It didn't take long for Holly to catch up to Alex. They ran side by side and kept on running, long after they'd left the others far behind.

"Tonight, I'm happy. Really, truly happy for the first time ever. And I know I don't have to be afraid anymore."

She sent the message to Alex and saw him glance her way in approval.

And she was happy.

Holly felt the night wind ripple along her back. She felt it stir her blood. She felt it awake the sleeping Power inside her.

And she knew she'd found her place. It was right here, at Alex's side.

THE SPELLBINDING DEBUT

Leslie Rule

WHISPERS FROM THE GRAVE

Two girls separated by a century—
yet bound by a haunting legacy

"Harrowing... Leslie Rule is a pure storyteller."
—John Saul

"Intricate plotting...unique, dual-
dimensional suspense."
—Lois Duncan

While exploring the family's attic, Jenna
discovers the tattered diary of Rita, a girl very
much like herself, who was murdered 100 years
ago. And the more Jenna delves into Rita's
shocking diary, the more she feels her fate has
already been decided. Because Rita's history is
repeating itself through Jenna...moment by
horrifying moment.

A Berkley paperback coming in June